SINFUL LITTLE BETRAYAL

A BILLIONAIRE ROMANCE

MIKA LANE

HEADLANDS PUBLISHING

CHAPTER 1

NARA

"You are *not* my husband, Simon. Stop telling people that."

"Nara dear, but I *am* your husband. And I will tell anyone I please that I'm. Your. Husband. Understand?"

Could I have hated someone more at that moment? I swallowed hard. I couldn't let my sort-of ex know how he rattled me, and yet *I* knew *he* knew he was getting under my skin. Successfully.

I took a deep breath. "I don't know why you are making this so hard, Simon. We agreed that as soon as you got your US citizenship, we'd start on the divorce."

I lowered my voice so my whole office wouldn't hear.

He chuckled like the smug fuck that he was. "Darling. Darling. Now, you *know* what you have to do if you want to cast me off so badly. 'Course that one night in London…well, it didn't seem like you wanted to ever leave my side. Or should I say, my *cock*?"

1

Mistake of a lifetime.

We'd been in London, his hometown, taking fake pictures to prepare for our big, fake US Immigration and Naturalization Service interview where we were going to fake being in love.

Simon had hired a friend to drive us to several different locations—with wardrobe changes—to take photos that would show how in love we were and that we would never, ever try to fool the INS. People did it all the time he'd assured me, and there was ten thousand dollars in it for me.

Good news all around.

Except for the one night I drank too much and ended up in bed with said future faux husband.

That had not been part of the deal. While he had that awesome British accent that Americans love, he also had bad teeth, a pasty complexion, and was at least two inches shorter than I.

And yet, I'd fucked him.

Oh, to do things over. But I'd needed that money. I'd been working on developing my software app for three long years with little income. Crashing on my best friend's couch was getting old. Really old.

That's when I answered a Craigslist ad to marry someone for a green card. It had sounded easy at the time, just like that adorable 90's movie *Green Card*, I told myself.

And now I was stuck with the bastard.

"Simon," I said with all the patience I could muster, "that was a fun night. It really was."

I choked on the biggest lie I'd ever told.

Truth was, I remembered nothing of our tryst, and that was just fine with me.

But I could hear him smiling through the phone. How I wished I could smack the grin off his face.

I continued, "But sweetie…"

I could almost hear him puffing his chest out.

Surely, logic would work. "We've taken care of business. We both got what we wanted. I'm grateful for that. And now, it's time to honor the last piece of our agreement."

How could he argue with that?

"I'll tell you what," he said as if he hadn't heard a word I'd just said. "My latest offer still stands. If you repay me the ten grand, I'll disappear out of your life forever. We'll annul the marriage and go on about our business like it never happened."

My face burned, and my hands shook. "Look. I helped you get your green card. You're in. You're as good as American, thanks to me. I earned that ten grand, I lied for you, married you, and even fucked you—"

"That was only one time—"

"*That's not the point*," I hissed. "You need to forget about extorting money from me. Give it up. It's not gonna happen. I don't have ten grand to give you even if I wanted to."

A migraine circled my head like a vulture looking for a meal. *Not now*, I begged. I needed my wits about me.

"Oh, Nara," Simon crooned, "we all know your software company has grown nicely. I'm sure you could write a check right now and be done with it."

Where did he get that kind of information? I'd been

breaking my back over my Mommy Knows for years. Yes, we were starting to get a little press. Yes, we were attracting the eye of potential customers and investors. But that didn't mean I had two nickels to rub together.

Because we didn't.

We were waiting for investors to come through, and until they did, the company was surviving off a line of credit. And getting perilously close to maxing that out. If we didn't get an infusion of cash soon, I had no idea what I'd do.

"Let me make this very clear," he said. "If you do not come up with the money I'm asking for, I will make sure all your current and future investors know you committed the felony of defrauding the INS. That will speak volumes about your character, and no one will touch your company with a ten-foot pole. And, I will not make it easy to divorce me."

He paused for effect.

"So, darling, what will it be?"

The migraine was no longer circling. It had landed with a crash, feasting on my poor little brain. Eyes closed, I rummaged through my desk for a pill, the only thing that would save my day. But it's hard to find things with closed eyes.

I said slowly and steadily, "I do not have ten thousand dollars. And if you ruin my company or me, there is even less chance that I ever will. You know that. You'd be sabotaging yourself."

It seemed he was thinking, due to the momentary silence.

"I want that money. I'll give you a month. I don't care

how you get it. Take a cash advance on one of your credit cards, for god's sake," he said.

A movement caught my eye, and I turned toward the opening of my office-that-was-really-a-cubicle.

Joi—my best friend, founding partner, and chief financial officer—stood in the doorway.

Like the rest of us, she wasn't getting paid much either, so she spent most of her days chasing after investors so that she someday would. I held up a *wait a minute* finger and turned back to my call.

"Simon, I have a meeting to run to. We'll continue this conversation later."

"I wouldn't wait too long—"

I hung up on the asshole.

No, I could never have hated someone more.

CHAPTER 2

BRODIE

"Mary, please slow down. I can't understand you. Take a deep breath and tell me what's going on." My hotel's long-time housekeeper was getting close to hyperventilating.

Her hair was pulled back into the severe knot that all our maids wore, and her top lip quivered.

"Mr. Brodie, I saw something in the penthouse suite. It was…terrible." The tears started.

Christ, what had she seen? A dead body?

But I shouldn't joke about something like that. People committed suicide in hotels all the time.

"Mary, sweetie, let's sit down over here." I put an arm around her shoulder and led her to one of the club chairs in my office. I sat opposite her.

"Oh, Mr. Brodie. I don't know if I can say it." She picked at the edges of her apron.

If she didn't spit it out soon, I'd just go up to the penthouse and see what the frig was going on. In fact, I might was well just do that.

I stood to go.

She blurted out, "Mr. Joel and Miss Pam were in there. Together. Doing…" She waved her hand around.

Apparently, she thought her hand wave was the universal sign for fucking, but no matter. I got the picture. Loud and clear.

I put my hands on Mary's shoulders. "Thank you for telling me. I really appreciate it. Now, why don't you relax here until you feel better? I'll have Trudy bring you some water."

I was gonna kill Joel.

I flew out of my office and down the hall. Before I barged in and launched into my tirade, I laughed at the sign on his office door.

Joel Fox, General Manager

General manager my ass. The dickhead wouldn't have a job if not for me.

"Joel, you in there?" I rapped my knuckles on the door.

There was of rustling from the other side. "Brodie, c'mon in, man."

Yeah, he sounded all cool and shit. Wait till I got ahold of him.

I flew in and slammed the door. Joel was adjusting his necktie. His shirt was wrinkled, and he'd missed a belt loop. Jesus, he couldn't even hide the evidence. Might as well have been walking around with his dick hanging out.

"Dude, were you in the penthouse suite *again*? No,

don't answer that. Because I *know* you were." I paced the room. "And you're fucking *Pam*? Are you kidding me?"

His head whipped around. "What's wrong with Pam?"

"That's not the point! You shouldn't fuck anyone at work, especially not on the premises, and especially not in the freaking penthouse suite."

He had nothing to say.

"And you gave Mary from housekeeping a goddamn heart attack. You know how straight-laced and religious she is. She's probably a goddamn virgin."

I quit pacing and whipped back around toward Joel.

He was trying not to laugh. I hated when he did that.

"Look, asshole, it's not funny. If the Dickhead Twins found out, I could be in a heap of trouble."

Joel shrugged in a lame attempt toward support. "They won't know. Don't worry." He had the nerve to lean back in his chair with his hands behind his head. Not a care in the world.

So, I put my hands on his desk and got in his face. "Next time you have the urge to screw Pam or anyone else from work, *go to another fucking hotel*!"

"But Brodie—"

I missed whatever he said after that, because I was out the door and halfway down the hall. My admin, Trudy, caught up to me.

"What's up, T?"

"Phone call," she said in her usual efficient way. I couldn't live without her. She'd been my dad's admin for years, and now she was mine. Like a second mother.

"Who is it?"

"Steve and Hardy, calling from Minneapolis." She

raised an eyebrow.

She knew me well.

The Dickhead Twins.

How could so much be so shitty, so early in the day?

"Want me to tell them you're out?" she asked.

It was tempting…

"Nah. I gotta take it. Thanks." I returned to my office, glad to see Mary had recovered and gone. One of her snotty tissues had fallen to the middle of the floor. The expensively carpeted floor. Much as I wanted to, I couldn't ask Trudy to pick it up. So I did.

I pressed the speaker on my desk phone to speak to the W and E of HWE, LLC—Harcourt, Wooten, and Evershire, the partnership we'd formed to run the hotel after my dad had royally screwed over their dads. I was working to make amends and pay them back, but they still treated me like I was a criminal every chance they got.

"Gentlemen," I said with as much fake cheer as I could muster.

"Hey, Brodie," they said unison.

I cleared my throat. I hated this part. "Hey, good to hear from you. Say, you guys give any thought to the San Francisco expansion I brought up a couple weeks ago?"

"Oh yeah. What was the deal with that?" one of them asked.

Sure, like they didn't remember. I'd only been bringing it up with them every time we spoke for the last six months.

"Hardy—" That *was* Hardy, wasn't it? They sounded so much alike. "I gave you numbers last week on what I think we could do with a property in San Francisco. The place is a convention and vacation heaven. It's always jam packed with people."

"Oh right," one of them said as if he'd forgotten.

Phony bastards. I clicked and unclicked the clasp on my gold Rolex, like I always did when irritated.

"Yeah, well, Steve and I have decided against that," Hardy said.

Had someone just poured molten lead into my stomach? Because that's how I felt.

Stay calm.

"Geez, guys, I'm really disappointed to hear that."

"Good idea, but impossible to execute on. There are more hotel rooms than ever in Frisco. We can't risk a property with a low or even average occupancy rate."

Narrow-minded assholes. Wouldn't know an opportunity if it bit them in the ass. And *no one* says *Frisco*.

I kept my voice friendly. It wasn't easy. "Hey, if it's okay with you two, I'd like to discuss this more. I feel like it's a great opportunity, and I know how we all hate to leave money on the table."

I wasn't ready to let it go, not by a long shot.

"Ya know, Brodie, your best opportunity is to keep your head down in New York City with Hotel Vertigo. Your numbers are getting better every month."

Okay then. Condescending prick. That's why I called them the Dickhead Twins.

"Yeah guys, they're getting better because I know how to run a successful fucking hotel," I barked.

"Hey now, let's not get bitchy. We just told ya you're doing great. Keep it up."

"Well, I gotta run," one of them said.

"Yeah, me too. Bye!" the other said.

Thank god they were in another state. Kept me from strangling the assholes.

My shitty mood must have been clear to anyone who saw me that day. The hotel staff gave me wide berth as I stormed around the back office halls. The accountant even pushed her door shut as I walked by.

It wasn't the first time.

But when I emerged into the lobby—the breathtakingly beautiful lobby of the hotel my father opened when I was just a kid—I was all calm and composure.

I surveyed the room. All was under control. Just how I liked it. The bellmen were smiling and helping guests with their luggage, the concierge was scoring some last minute theater tickets for some delighted guests, and reception was checking people in at record speed. Even the gardener was trimming and watering so discretely that no one noticed him.

This is how you run a fucking hotel.

The head of housekeeping spotted me and approached with quick steps. Like my admin, Trudy, she'd been with the hotel for years, going back to my father's days.

"Mr. Harcourt, would you like to inspect a couple rooms now?" she asked.

Inspecting rooms was part of my daily ritual. I always checked out a couple random rooms to make sure the housekeeping staff were on top of it. Nothing puts a hotel out of business faster than dirty rooms. Once news like that hit the social media sites, word would spread like wildfire.

You know those hidden camera news stories where hotel maids wiped out used bathroom glasses with a dirty towel and set them back out for the next guest?

Over. My. Dead. Body.

"Yes, Jones. I'm ready for inspection. Let's start with the penthouse suite."

Her face dropped all semblance of color. For a moment, I thought she might faint.

"Um, well, um, Mr. Harcourt, the penthouse isn't ready just yet."

Of course it wasn't ready. Joel, the general manager, had just fucked Pam, the HR manager, there. Jones would have heard it from the freaked-out maid.

"Well, we both know that only the bed needs changing since no one—theoretically—spent the night there. What's the hold up?"

"Mary doesn't want to go back in there. So I need one of the other girls to clean it."

She hesitated.

"Or you know, I could clean it," she said quickly.

Good girl.

"You know I always say that everyone in management —myself included—is expected to be ready to jump in, no matter what the task. That's what keeps this hotel great," I said.

While I was tormenting poor Jones, I was able to keep an eye on everything else going on in the lobby. Not least of which was a hot-as-shit girl behind the reception desk.

Sonya something or other. And damn if she wasn't giving me the eye.

Last time she'd done that, I'd gotten the blowie of a lifetime. Right next to the copy machine in the office behind the front desk.

I didn't care who knew.

I'd tuned out whatever Jones was blathering on about. I gave her a nice pat on the back. "Thank you, Jones. I'll be checking out those rooms later."

I headed for the front desk.

"But sir," Jones called after me, "there's one more thing—"

There was always one more thing with her. Such a time-suck.

With my gaze glued to Sonya and her great tits, I waved over my shoulder. "Jones, we'll finish this later."

I waited until Sonya finished with the guest she was helping.

"Hi, Sonya, how are you this morning?"

The other person behind reception, a sprightly gay guy named Scott, minded his own business and scurried away. Bless his heart.

Her face lit up. She was even more gorgeous when she smiled. "Mr. Harcourt, hi." She blushed.

And my dick twitched. Something about a bashful babe who could suck cock just killed me.

I said nothing further. I didn't need to. I walked to the end of the long reception desk and used my key card for the door to the back office. Just like last time, she met me there by the copy machine. We closed the door.

My morning was about to improve.

CHAPTER 3

NARA

I hated being late. And the irony was, I was *always* late. It was in my DNA. I was just not made for being early. Or even on time, for that matter.

"Ouch, dammit!" Oooh, did I just say that?

"I'm so sorry, Miss Kincaid. I'll be more careful."

A model-esque saleswoman entered the wedding shop dressing room where I was acting as a human pincushion. She was dressed in head-to-toe black. Even the bun secured at the nape of her neck was black.

"Now, doesn't that dress look lovely on you," she purred. No doubt she said that to everyone getting fitted for a marginally attractive bridesmaid dress that they'd never wear again.

She waited. Guess she was expecting a reply.

"Yes, it is nice." I sighed, looking down at the sweeping skirt. How was I going to walk in this?

"It's better than the pink and purple confections I've

worn in my other friends' weddings. Who, by the way, are now all divorced."

Her expression changed to one of extreme distaste, as if someone had stepped in dog poop and tracked it all over her white carpet. She hightailed it out of there, leaving me with the smirking seamstress.

The woman pinning my dress felt my pain, I could tell.

Before I could escape the shop, I was informed I'd be charged for the balance of my bridesmaid dress, having previously only paid the deposit. I handed over my credit card, fingers crossed the charge would go through.

"Thank you Miss Kincaid," she said, handing the card back. "You can pick up your dress next week—"

But I didn't hear the rest. My Uber ride was waiting out front.

I ran out the door, slipping into the car without my usual security measures like making sure the make, model, and license plate matched what the Uber phone app said would be coming for me.

But it was quickly obvious there was nothing to worry about. If I didn't know better, I would swear I'd just been picked up by Betty White's younger sister. Betty White of *Golden Girls* fame.

"Hi, sweetie. What were you doin' in that bridal shop? You getting married?" She steered into traffic like a champ.

"My best friend Joi is getting married in a few weeks. I'm in the wedding."

"Isn't that nice. She pick an ugly dress for you?" She cackled.

"Actually, it's not too bad. It's midnight blue, very simple."

"So you can wear it again, right? Just like they all say!" More cackling.

She shook her white, permed head. It was a wonder she could see over the steering wheel.

"I remember my first wedding, back in 1955. Damn if we didn't wear ugly dresses back then. We looked like cake toppers. And shit, I was a virgin for my first husband…" She jabbered the whole way across town while I checked my phone in the back seat.

We pulled up in front of the Hotel Vertigo. I wouldn't have minded riding around with this ace driver longer, but duty called. I tipped her a ten and ran inside.

"Where's the auction?" I breathlessly asked the concierge.

He pointed at the giant sign I'd just blown past, the one that said "Avenue A Fundraiser" in huge letters. I followed the arrow on it and headed down a corridor.

I quietly crept into the packed ballroom to avoid attracting attention. The fundraising auction was well underway, and I could see my assistant, Mimi, up in the front row.

I sent her a text to check in.

u bidding for me?

u bet, boss!

who u bidding on?

guy stage right. tall. expensive suit.

ok. thnks.

I fished out my glasses so I could see from the back of the room. This was another of those trendy New York fundraisers where certain desirable men and women were "auctioned" for dates, with all the proceeds going to charity.

The Avenue A homeless shelter was a great organization, and one I'd always supported. Bidding on a date wasn't really my idea of fun, but to raise money for a good cause, I could be coerced.

Apparently, I'd missed the part of the auction where they sold off the women. Something about that was skeevy in a way that it wasn't with the guys. But I pushed the thought out of my head.

There were six nice-enough looking men on stage, lined up in chairs like an old episode of *The Dating Game*.

I mean, you couldn't auction someone with running sores, could you? This was a charity fundraiser, after all.

And wouldn't you know, the guy Mimi had pointed out to me via text looked like a douche. Figures. The guys in these auction-a-date fundraisers were always douches to one degree or another.

The things I did for charity.

"Nara! How lovely to see you!"

If I'd just ridden with Betty White's younger sister, this was her cousin. Another 80-something cutie with a tight perm, veneers, and a pushup bra.

"Mrs. Dolan, how nice to see you."

She ran several of Manhattan's big, high-profile fundraisers, and had dragged me into this one. She was a champ at separating people from their money.

Just look at me.

"Thank you for coming, my dear. The shelter so appreciates your support. Tell me, what is it your company's technology does again? I think you told me once before…"

She must have been hard of hearing from how loudly she spoke; several people turned to give us the stink eye until they realized they were dissing an octogenarian.

I steered her away from the crowd. "We make an app that notifies a mom—or dad—on their phone the moment their baby has a dirty diaper."

She looked at me like I was speaking Chinese. But her bright smile never wavered.

"Oh, an app. I think I've heard of those." She wandered away.

Which was fine with me. I needed to text Mimi to make sure she wasn't spending me into the poor house. I would pay for a douchebag in the name of charity and to help out the adorable Mrs. Dolan. But I wasn't going to sacrifice my shoe habit. Such as it was.

There was a shuffle at the front of the ballroom. The auctioneer on stage appeared very pleased with himself for having "sold" some guy named Bill or Bud—or was it Brodin?—for the highest amount in today's action.

And the lucky sucker who got him?

Me.

The room broke out in applause, and my phone blew up with texts from Mimi, quite pleased with herself.

I thanked her. What else could I say? She'd done what I'd asked her to do. Now, all I had to do was pay for the date, suffer through some time with him, and call it a day.

I'd done my duty for the Avenue A homeless shelter and Mrs. Dolan until their next fundraiser rolled around.

There was a tug on my sleeve.

Mrs. Dolan was beaming. "Nara, you got a good one, I tell ya. They saved the best for last! Now, let me take you up front to meet your new date."

She started moving toward the stage before she realized I wasn't following. "Sweetie? C'mon." She gestured with her head. The tight perm curls didn't move.

Ugh. I'd meet the guy on our date, and not a moment sooner.

"I need to get back to work. I'll follow up with my date later." I glanced at my watch for effect.

Where was Mimi? Maybe she could go on the date *for* me...

"Well, okay. If you insist. But I've known the young man since he was little. He's a nice guy, I tell you."

Nah. I was good.

Mimi finally appeared at my side, red curls bouncing. Like always, she was the picture of efficiency.

"Thanks, Mrs. Dolan," I said, bending to give her a quick hug. She smelled like powder. "I'll let you know how the date goes. But I have to head out right now."

Mimi sensed something in my urgency. That's why she was my assistant. I'd be lost without her and her sixth sense.

"Nara! Our Uber is here! Gotta go!" She took me by the elbow, thank god.

"I'll be in touch soon," I called over my shoulder as we ran.

As we flew out the door, I saw my future date walking around like a puffed up peacock.

It was gonna be one fun date.

CHAPTER 4

BRODIE

How did I get roped into these bachelor auctions?

New York was full of rich, single men. Why did I always get sucked in?

I was in another shitty mood, the joy of Sonya's earlier blowie having worn off long ago. And a redhead in the front row had bid on me like some sort of psycho, driving up the price to outbid all the other women there.

The crowd disbursed as the auctioneer gathered up his papers from behind the podium. He looked like Colonel Sanders with his white hair and goatee.

"Well, Mr. Harcourt," he said to me, "another successful auction in your great hotel."

The ballroom cleared with all the generous supporters of the Avenue A homeless shelter having headed back to work, out to lunch, or to the gym.

The smell of roses and a light tap grabbed my attention.

"Brodie, dear, I had hoped to introduce you to the lovely young lady who *bought* you," Mrs. Dolan, the tiny, silver-haired fundraising chair said with a giggle.

She relished selling people. Little perv. The tiny but top-notch New York money hound led the fundraising efforts of some of the city's biggest charities.

But now it seemed she was also a matchmaker of sorts. No wonder she loved these date auctions.

"Sadly, honey, she had to get back to work. So you'll have to meet her on your actual date!" She patted my shoulder to comfort me.

I just didn't need another date with a lonely nutjob who had too many cats. The last auction winner I had to take out told me within the first five minutes of our meeting that she wanted to have three kids. She had also kept looking at my crotch.

No thanks.

My mode of operation with these dates, which I seemed to have to deal with a couple times a year, was to have good old Trudy, my admin, call me forty-five minutes into the date with an "emergency."

I'd throw some money on the table and get the hell out. Worked like a charm.

The things I did for charity.

And now I had another to deal with. But it was okay. I had my system. Trudy had my back, just like she'd always had my dad's when he was running the hotel.

But poor Mrs. Dolan was disappointed that my auction "winner" had bolted. I could give a crap, person-ally, but I felt sad for her, a woman I'd known nearly all my life, who'd stood by my dad's side during the good times and bad. I'd do just about anything for her.

Thus, my hotel not only hosted most of the fundraisers she ran, but I was also pimped out for her bachelor auctions. Every time. It was a pain in the ass, but I liked the idea of helping her *and* raising money for a good cause.

Kill two birds with one stone.

"I'm sure she'll be in touch with me soon," I told her.

"I hope so, sweetheart. She paid a lot of money for you." She cackled like it was the funniest thing she'd ever said, and scanned the crowd.

"You know, I have another young lady for you to meet."

Shit.

"And there she is." She waved frantically, but was so short no one would ever see her. So she hollered.

Who knew that little thing's vocals packed such a punch?

"Janine! Janine, over here!" She kept waving and probably would have jumped if she hadn't been so old.

Great. She'd found her Janine, who came rushing toward her with a smile.

But when Janine set her eyes on me, her smile fell. Fortunately, Mrs. Dolan was oblivious.

"Brodie, I'd like you to meet my granddaughter, Janine." She looked back and forth between us, beaming, looking for a much hoped-for spark.

But there would be no spark. At least, not a romantic one.

Janine was the woman I'd fucked two weeks ago. And had never called.

Oops.

That's the price to be paid when you're a guy like me. I extended my hand.

"Brodie. Hello. Long time." She ignored my hand.

Mrs. Dolan clapped her hands. I wonder if she knew her granddaughter fucked on the first date.

"You two know each other! What a small world. Isn't this fantastic!"

"I hope you've been well," I told her.

I did hope she'd been well. I had no problem with her. It was just that there were so many beautiful women in Manhattan. No reason to settle down with just one.

"You didn't call me."

Oh, shit. She was going there, right in front of her nana.

Mrs. Dolan's wrinkly little brow was all furrowed.

Time for my exit. I glanced at my watch. "Oh cripes, I have a meeting that started five minutes ago. Good to see you, Janine. Mrs. Dolan." I bent to give the old lady a peck on the cheek.

I got the hell out of there, hoping Janine wouldn't tell her grandmother what a prick I could be.

But honestly, Mrs. Dolan could probably give a shit as long as she could pimp me out.

Back in my office, I called my stepbrother, Dalt, in Sausalito, an awesome artsy little town just outside San Francisco.

"Yo, Bro," he hollered.

Dalt was the only one who could call me that.

"Dude. How's Sausalito and the art world?"

I pushed my office door closed and looked around. God, Trudy kept this place nice. I would annihilate it by leaving papers and other crap all over the place, and she'd have it straightened out in the time it took me to take a piss.

Seagulls screeched on the other end of the line. Was that bastard at the beach?

"Yeah, had an art show last week and sold all but one of my paintings. I'm at Stinson Beach right now, about to go over to Noelle's tavern."

"Damn! Where's my painting, man?"

Dalt laughed. "I'm working on it."

"I just got out of another one of those bachelor auction things."

"What? You always get sucked into those. Some group here, I think it was called the Guardsmen, tried to recruit me. I told them *hell no*. But I did write a check to their charity."

"Well, I didn't get off quite that easy. You know Mrs. Dolan."

"She's the one who helped your dad out, right?"

"Yeah, good memory. She runs the things. Hey, how's Noelle?"

"Gorgeous as ever." He laughed again. "Really working her ass off in both the tavern and doing massage at Devi's

Bliss. I don't know how she does it, dude. I just get tired watching her. So what's up with things in the Big Apple?"

"My business partners are still shitting on my idea of expanding to San Francisco. They say the market is saturated," I explained.

"They're dead wrong. Let me see if I can introduce you to some investors here. The Tenderloin is being developed like crazy, and it's adjacent to downtown. Perfect location."

"Dalt, that would be awesome. Thanks."

"All right. I gotta run."

"See ya," I said.

I loved that guy.

CHAPTER 5

"Mimi, can't you get me out of this?" I whined. "I don't want to go on a date with a guy from a bachelor auction."

I could whine to Mimi. That's how close we were.

The Uber ride back to the office was taking *forever*. Where was my Betty White look-alike when I needed her?

"No, I cannot. You agreed to this, and now you have to follow through."

She might have been my assistant, but half the time, I felt like she was the boss. In a good way.

"You go for me," I insisted. "The guy will never know. Just pretend to be me. He saw *you* bidding on him. He'll be expecting a redhead."

Mimi raised an eyebrow at me. "*Page Six* from the *New York Post* wants to interview you about bachelor/bachelorette auctions. In fact, they want to see if they can come on your first date."

"What? Oh my god. *Page Six*, the gossip column? First, they cannot. And second, by saying *first date*, they are implying there will be subsequent dates. Which is not going to happen."

She shrugged. "Okay. I'll let them know." She got quiet and looked out the window.

"What?" I asked. "Do you think I should let the most infamous gossip column in all of New York in on my private life?"

"It could be good publicity for Mommy Knows."

My company. My baby.

"Wow. Good thinking, Mimi. Yeah, maybe we should set that up. I mean, I don't know about them accompanying us on the actual date, but I can talk to them about it after."

Mimi looked at me with approval. "Okay. I'll get in touch with my contact there. You just talk about the company as much as you can. You know how many bored stay-at-home moms with a lot of money read *Page Six*?"

Maybe these auctions were not such a pain in the butt after all. "God, Mimi. Will you remind me to give you a raise some day?"

She laughed. "I will remind you. As soon as we start turning a profit."

Amen, sister.

When pulled up in front of our office building, Mimi took off to get our favorite lunch from the corner vendor —hotdogs smothered in mustard and relish. And of course, Diet Cokes.

The vendor had a crush on Mimi and always gave us an extra dollop of sauerkraut.

In all the morning's excitement—getting fitted for a dress I didn't want and buying a date with a guy I didn't want—I'd missed a call from the asshole, fake husband Simon.

His voicemail message was predictable.

"Nara, darling, I hope you've been thinking hard about my proposal. I want my ten grand back, and the clock is ticking—"

I deleted his message without hearing the rest. He wouldn't even be in the damn country if it weren't for me. He had a career, a great apartment. Probably an occasional date, although I couldn't imagine with whom.

But if he ratted me out, didn't he realize he was risking his *own* well-being in addition to mine? If it got to the INS, he was the one who'd be deported. Not *me*.

I Googled *sham marriage INS*. And the blood drained from my face.

Up to five years in prison. Up to $250,000 in fines.

Dear god.

But he wouldn't rat me out. He couldn't be that stupid. Or self-destructive. I mean, he'd be imprisoned, fined, or both, *and* kicked out of the country. All for ten thousand dollars.

Back when I agreed to marry Simon, I was desperate for money. And I knew other people around the city doing the same thing—earning some quick cash by marrying someone who needed a green card; the non-US citizen would get one once married to a US citizen.

In fact, one of my girlfriends married an adorable French guy. I'd figured, how tough could it be? And it seemed easier than donating eggs.

Just as I was dreaming about Simon crossing the street and being leveled by a city bus, my cell rang. The phone screen said *Mom*.

"Hey there," I answered.

"Hi honey. It's Mom."

"I know it's you, Mom. My phone recognizes your number."

"Oh right, you told me that last time."

"Why don't you let me get you a nice new phone? Get rid of that old flip phone."

She sighed. "I know you're really into technology and all that, but I'm perfectly happy with my old phone. It works great. I don't do that texting thing, and I don't know how to Facebook, so I'm doing fine."

Ugh. How the mother of a software developer like me could be so dismissive of technology was baffling.

"Okay, Mom."

She sighed. "How's the company, sweetie? Are people catching on to your product? You know, the idea of being *told* when your child has a dirty diaper as opposed to the way we did it in my day *does* sound…like it has potential. Much better than waiting till you smell something awful or the kid starts wailing. I suppose."

Fortunately, she couldn't see my eyes roll.

"Yes, Mom. People are starting to learn about us. We have several mothers testing the software right now, so far with good feedback."

What I didn't explain was that the app sometimes had trouble telling the difference between number one and number two, which was vital to our success. Whether the mess was solid or liquid had a big impact on a mom's approach to keeping her kid's butt clean.

The things I'd been learning about…and the diapers I'd had the unfortunate luck to get a whiff of…

"So, honey, you know your fifteen-year high school reunion is just around the corner."

Oh shit. *That* was why she was calling?

No way I would not be attending that fiasco. Hell to the *no*. Just what I needed, to be reminded of the shit show that was my high school life.

"You're coming back home for it, right?" So much hope.

"No, I'm not. I don't want to see those people." Nor did I want to return to the horrendous podunk town I'd grown up in.

"What do you mean by *those people*? You grew up with *those people*. They were your friends your entire life until you left town. And besides, don't you want to see *me*?"

"'Course I want to see you. I'll get you a ticket to New York anytime you like."

She didn't fly, which was probably just as well because I could really only afford to get her a bus ticket. And she loved the bus.

Mimi dropped off my hotdog. Mmmm. Salty New York deliciousness. I nodded my thanks, and she disappeared back to her own cube.

"I don't understand why you are so opposed to coming back home and seeing your old friends. You needn't be embarrassed you've never gotten married."

It was so cute, her assumption that I didn't want to come back because I was single. Maybe she'd feel better if

I told her about my sham marriage to Simon. In her world, that would probably be better than nothing.

Going to the reunion as a single woman was the *least* of my worries.

"Mom, you know I don't fit in there anymore. I have a new life. What could I possibly have in common with them?"

"Now, I don't know why you think you're so much better than those people, but just because you went to New York and started your own company doesn't mean you're anything special."

Gee, thanks.

"Expect a call from the reunion committee," she continued.

"What? How? Mom, you didn't give them my contact info, did you? I expressly asked you *not* to do that."

"Sorry, but you'll some day regret neglecting your old friends back home. I gave them your phone number and address."

Note to self, do not answer any unknown callers.

"I asked you not to—"

"I *know* Becca would love to see you."

The mention of Becca really crashed my mood even more so than the stupid dating auction and Simon's extortion. And the ugly bridesmaid's dress.

"Oh, Mom." I groaned. There would just never be any meeting of the minds on this.

But I couldn't go back. For one, what would I possibly talk about?

How I was no longer the slut I was in high school?

How I'd gotten it together, gone to college, and started my own company in New York City?

Becca, on the other hand, had had four kids before she was thirty. Our lives had gone in radically different directions, just as I always knew they would.

But the guilt of leaving her, my mom, and the town itself gutted me. I'd worked so hard to get out, and yet I felt crappy about it.

"Hey, Mom, I have a meeting. I gotta go. Talk to you later. Love you. Bye."

I waited for her to return the sentiment, but all I heard was *bye*.

CHAPTER 6

BRODIE

Exactly two weeks after the auction, I grabbed a ride uptown in the hotel limo. Time to meet the crazy redhead who'd bid on me at the Avenue A fundraiser.

Seriously, what chick would spend so much for one lousy date? I could understand why the guys did it—there was always the possibility of getting a lay out of it. But the women who bid on guys? Were they out for a lay, too? And it's not that my "winner" was a bad-looking woman. On the contrary, that red hair and those freckles were damn hot.

But experience told me the women who were into this were on the whacky side.

My admin Trudy was briefed, god love her, and she knew the drill. I'd send her a text just as soon as the "date" got started. She'd call me forty-five minutes later with some sort of "hotel emergency." I'd escape.

No harm, no foul.

The driver wove through the heavy rush-hour traffic but we were moving at a snail's pace. I still had plenty of time to get there, but I hated being late. And I hated late people, too.

Last week, I'd gotten a brief email from Nara, the woman who'd won me in the auction.

Usually, these women, once they set up our date, would send me a flurry of emails telling me more about themselves than I ever wanted to know. Maybe it was to break the ice—who knew. Either way, I would dutifully read them so our forty-five minute date wasn't spent just staring at each other.

As always, the dates had Googled me beforehand, finding that I was the owner of the most exclusive and in-demand hotel in all of Manhattan. They liked that. They liked my money.

But if they really dug deep, they'd find the story of my father. That part, they didn't like.

They might allude to Dad and his crimes, digging around for more info, or to get my take on the whole fiasco. But they were most always too polite to really persist in finding out more about the embezzling bastard.

And it wasn't like I needed reminding. I was paying for his sins every day of my life, trying to make things right with the people he swindled.

Anyway, Nara's email was different. Short, sweet, to the point. Perfunctory. No facts or details about anything, much less her life. Maybe redheads were like that?

She'd written:

Hi, Brodie. Can you meet me at Bella Stella on Park next Thursday at five? Thanks, Nara

That was it. No blathering on about her boring-ass job or that she had a really cheap, rent-controlled apartment, or how every Christmas Eve for the last ten years she went caroling with her friends.

Which was fine. She could do the talking. Forty-five minutes for charity. I could deal with that.

As we crept along Park Avenue, I took the opportunity to check on the cleanliness of the hotel limo. I was stuck sitting there, so why not?

And don't you know…there was a condom wrapper stuffed down the seat back.

Goddammit.

Why did I look? Now I'd be pissed for the rest of the evening. Better I'd found it than some A-list hotel guest.

On the other hand, it was probably some goddamn A-list hotel guest who left it there to begin with.

Of course now that I found the wrapper, I couldn't help but wonder where the damn condom was.

Guess the asshole who used it had taken it with him. Nice of him.

I fired off a text to Trudy to make sure the limo went through a deep clean as soon as it was back in the garage.

The shit I dealt with.

A text came in from my stepbro, Dalt:

hey, i have some folks who want to discuss your san fran expansion. call me.

I texted back:

dude. on my way out. will call in the a.m.

Yeah, baby.

He knew my business partners were douches. Ever since my dad screwed the company, which was at the time owned by all our dads, the partners had been putting me through the ringer. They were basically pains in my ass whenever they got the chance. And they got the chance a lot.

Not that I really blamed them. My dad stole from their dads, straight up, and I was trying to make it right. But sometimes, they really tested my sense of obligation. They didn't give a crap about Hotel Vertigo. They just wanted payback.

The day they were repaid so I could get them the hell out of my life could not come soon enough.

According to an agreement worked out by the courts, *until* they were repaid, I had to run everything by them. I couldn't blow my nose without their permission. Which wouldn't have been so bad had they been decent businessmen with the ability to recognize an opportunity when they saw one.

But they'd only inherited their old man's money, and unfortunately no business sense.

I understood it—their dads had gotten swindled by mine, but no one was more tortured by it than me. They were angry and bitter, and seemed more interested in putting the hotel out of business than making it a success so they could get their due. Talk about cutting off your nose to spite your face.

But things might be different with Dalt's offer of help. He knew people in San Francisco who were both entrepreneurial and good investors.

People there were always looking for their next deal. They lived to take chances, more so than the folks I knew on the East Coast. And they *loved* hotels and restaurants.

It would be a brilliant move to expand the current New York property to San Francisco. 'Course I could always finance it myself, with my own investments, but it was always better to work with partners—as long as they were savvy business people.

It lent more legitimacy to the project.

Yes, with the right investors, I could just open something completely new and escape my shortsighted partners.

I had enough contacts in the entertainment biz to attract plenty of big name guests. Once I got those folks, the others always followed—key to making a hotel as hip and in-demand as possible.

Dalt and I hadn't become stepbrothers until we were in high school when my mom married his dad. But when the shit hit the fan, and my father had been exposed for all his crooked dealings, Dalt had stepped up to the plate to support me.

You don't forget something like that.

I'd worked for the company since I was a kid, but when it all went down and Dad had been arrested, I'd been left in charge. My head had spun from the press, the lawyers, and yes, death threats.

But Dalt had stood by me and even loaned me some cash when I was nearly broke; all the hotel's assets had been seized, and I was trying to pay all the bills out of my own savings.

Later, when the dust had settled and our accounts were unfrozen, I was able to pay him back and then some. I'd invested in *him*, and now, he was a well-known and successful artist.

Best thing I'd ever done.

At last the limo pulled up in front of the restaurant. I hadn't been to Stella Bella before but its Yelp reviews were decent. It didn't really matter, though.

It would be a quick in and out.

I was a few minutes early, so I went inside to start on a nice scotch on the rocks. Alcohol would help the forty-five minute date pass. Then Trudy would rescue me and I'd be on my way.

I sent the driver off to kill the better part of an hour, and smoothing out the wrinkles in my suit, headed for the door.

Bella Stella—what a corny name—was a typical New York City eatery, with an outside awning over the doorway and a couple sidewalk tables.

I entered the cozy space with exposed brick walls, heavy chandeliers, and a lit votive candle on every table. I settled in at the bar and watched the wait staff hustle through their last-minute dinner preparations.

At five minutes to the hour there was no sign of the redhead, but there was still time for her to be early, like me.

CHAPTER 7

NARA

Of course I ended up being late for my date with… what was his name? Oh yeah, Brodie something-or-other.

My team and I had been presenting Mommy Knows to some beta test customers, who were going to try it out for us on their babies. I'd lost track of time, and Mimi was off doing something else so hadn't been there to rein me in.

Not many people get as enthusiastic as we did when it came to talking about dirty diapers. It was a rare skill.

Luckily, Bella Stella was right around the corner from our office. Actually, that's why I'd chosen it. I'd spent the money "buying" the date, so I figured I could pick the location. The guy hadn't had any objections; he'd replied to my invitation with an *okay*. I just hoped that during our time together, which I was going to make sure was short and sweet, he had something a little more interesting to say than that.

Because the restaurant was right around the corner from my office, the staff there knew me. It was our "place" when we wanted an after work drink or when we had investors to take to lunch. The food was good enough, like most Italian joints in the city, and when you went there often, it felt like home.

Before entering, I straightened out my skirt and smoothed down my hair. I don't know why, but I wanted to look nice. I also wanted to get the date over with so I could say I'd done it, and have something to report to the gossip machine at *Page Six*.

I wasn't going to give this guy the chance to say he'd been "bought" by some disheveled woman with lipstick on her teeth.

I slipped inside, tucking myself next to a booth by the door, staring at the back of a solo man at the bar. I figured it was him. The manager nodded to me from the kitchen where he was cooking something amazing-smelling.

The guy leaned on the bar, nursing some type of brown liquor. Probably a scotch, like every other master of the universe-wannabee in New York. His hair was nice and thick—I'd give him that—and he was wearing a suit. I guessed it was expensive from the fit.

Oh shit, he turned around and looked right at me.

Busted.

But strangely, he just turned back to the bar. Maybe he hadn't seen me? He looked at his watch and took another sip of his drink.

I waited longer. Of course, it was rude to be late, but I was curious and relished the thought of having someone I was quite sure was overly impressed with himself wait for little old me.

At twelve minutes after the hour—late, but not hideously so—I approached him. He turned at the sound of my clicking high heels, and I put on my best how-ya-doin smile.

I hadn't realized how good-looking he was until I got closer.

"My date, I presume?" I extended my hand.

He looked surprised as hell as he studied my face and hair. What was that all about? Did I look that bad? My hand flew up to check my hair.

"I'm Nara Kincaid."

"Hello, Nara, I'm Brodie Harcourt." He stood and took my hand as I climbed onto the barstool next to his. Chalk one up for good manners. And good lord, he was tall.

His phone vibrated, and he pulled it out of his jacket pocket. I spotted what I knew was a fancy watch. Some of the high roller investors we'd met with wore the same.

"Excuse me, I'm just gonna respond to my admin's text." He typed a couple words and set the device face down on the old wooden bar.

The bartender, who obviously knew me well, delivered a glass of pink bubbly.

He turned to Brodie, "Sir? Would you like a second Macallan?"

I knew it.

He nodded and turned back to me. "So, Nara, I have to be honest with you. I was expecting a redhead."

I couldn't help but belt out a laugh.

"Oh, right! My assistant got to the auction before I did

and bid on my behalf. I was running late. In fact, I asked her to handle this date for me, but she wouldn't have any part of it."

Oh shit. Did I just say that?

He smiled. Or was that a smirk? "And why'd you do that? Try to get her to take the date for you?"

Ugh.

"Oh gosh, I didn't mean any offense. It's just that I'm so busy—"

"Do you have a boyfriend or something? A husband?"

"No, no, it's not that," I sputtered.

"No?"

I yammered on. "You know, I mean, I didn't want to do this silly date thing. Who would? I'm happy to support the Avenue A homeless shelter, but Mrs. Dolan twisted my arm to bid on a date. I mean, who bids on a guy in a freaking auction?"

Ugh. Stop talking. Now.

His mouth dropped open, but he snapped it shut just as quickly. Jesus, what was wrong with me? I sucked down my drink and waved the bartender over for another glass of bubbly.

Anything to keep me from talking.

Brodie nodded slowly as if some profound understanding had washed over him. Like he'd realized I'm a big, huge bitch.

Christ.

"Look, I'm sorry. That was rude. I don't know why I said that."

My phone buzzed. Mimi! I texted her back.

b there soon just finishing up

I'd leave early. Who cared? I'd already done all the damage I could. And this was a big city. I'd never see the guy again.

But then there was the *Page Six* story. And possibly some free publicity for Mommy Knows. There were a lot of moms out there who were tired of sniffing their kid's butts…

And he was damn handsome, in that chiseled, dark-eyed, Ralph Lauren model sort of way. But it didn't matter. I wouldn't be seeing him after this one time. Although I did feel a little twinge in my core…

"So Mrs. Dolan strong armed you?" he asked.

"Yes, she did. Is that how she got you, too?"

I was trying to keep my words to a minimum. No more verbal diarrhea if I could help it.

He sipped his scotch. "Oh yeah. I've known her a long time."

"No kidding! She's a little cutie, isn't she? How do you know her?"

He looked down for a sec. "Old family friend," he said, looking back up. "How do you know her?"

"My company volunteers several times a year at the shelter. They invited me to a fundraising meeting, and I met her there." I laughed. "She sank her claws into me pretty hard and hasn't let go."

The smile returned to his face. "She's like that, isn't she?" His phone vibrated on the bar, but he ignored it. "What kind of company do you work for?"

"A small tech firm called Mommy Knows."

"Mommy Knows…I can't say I know that one. What's the product?"

Of course, he didn't know about it. He wasn't a parent saddled with poopy diapers.

"We have a software app. It links to a mom's—or dad's—iPhone and lets them know when their kid has a dirty diaper. So instead of waiting for the baby to start crying, you know right away. You can even have babysitters use it."

His eyes widened. Then he threw his head back and laughed. I couldn't blame him. The concept always sounded absurd at first. But explain it to any parent of a kid in diapers, and there was immediate understanding. It was like lights turning on. One mom I had explained it to had actually gotten tears in her eyes.

"Wow. That's quite a concept. What do you do there?"

"I'm the founder and CEO."

His eyes widened again. I was familiar with this part…"You're kidding!"

"Yup. I'm a software developer." Here it comes…

"You're a tech CEO. Wow! But you look so…"

"Yeah, I know." I was wearing my usual black pencil skirt, silk blouse, and sky-high pumps. On the other hand, most of my staff usually looked like they'd just rolled out of bed.

"How'd you come up with the concept? Do you have kids?"

My hand flew to my chest in mock horror. "God, no! I'd seen other moms sniffing their kid's diapers to see if they needed changing. I thought that was just gross, and I wanted to come up with a better solution."

"So you're a software developer." I noticed him sitting up straighter in his seat.

"Yup. Sure am."

Mimi would be expecting me, but I couldn't sneak a look at my watch. Too rude.

"What about you, Brodie? How'd you end up as one of Mrs. Dolan's victims?"

"Mrs. Dolan used to do charity work with my dad."

I nodded. "Well, that was a gorgeous hotel, wasn't it?"

He nodded with enthusiasm. "Yes, thank you."

"What do you mean, thank you?" I asked.

"That was my hotel. Hotel Vertigo."

Now it was my turn to be surprised. "No kidding! Great place."

It really had been quite beautiful. And elegant.

"Thanks," he said, nodding. "It's been in the family for a long time. My dad's no longer involved, so I'm in charge now. We're doing okay for ourselves."

So he was a hotelier. That was no pretty boy job. He probably worked his ass off and did long hours, holidays, weekends. Well, well.

But still. Didn't one have to be conceited to be auctioned for charity?

Just then, my phone chirped. It knew it was Mimi, letting me know it was time to excuse myself and go.

Only I wasn't ready yet.

CHAPTER 8

BRODIE

I'll be damned. Nara, my auction date, wasn't a desperate, lonely cat lady after all.

She was a freaking tech CEO. And she didn't even bid on me—her damn redheaded assistant did.

There I was, bracing myself for another charity date, and I was met with this gorgeous woman in clothes possibly more expensive than mine, who was not the least bit impressed with me or anything about me.

Why did I feel like the joke was on me?

At least she liked my hotel. And I totally dug how she blurted out her true feelings about the auction. *That* was worth the price of admission.

She pulled her phone out and typed a quick message, then slipped it back into her bag.

"Sorry 'bout that. My assistant's just checking in."

She turned her barstool toward me and crossed her

long legs. I wished she'd go to the ladies' room or something so I could really check her out. At such close range, my gaze could scarcely leave her face.

And what a face it was. Jesus. Bright blue eyes, black hair, and lips that curled into the most adorable, lopsided smile. A long-ish face that on anyone else might not have worked. But on her, it did. Beautifully.

If only all the women at those auctions were like her, I'd sign up for every damn one in town.

And she wanted to know more about my business. Not in an *I want to know how much money you're worth way*, but an *I'm interested in business* sort of way.

It got my dick hard. Smart girls did that for me, no doubt. And it wasn't that Manhattan wasn't full of brilliant women—it absolutely was. It was just that I rarely met one who…I don't know—didn't give a shit about me or my assets.

"Since you took over the hotel from your dad, how have you changed it?" she asked.

I'd given her the Cliffs Notes version—I couldn't tell her the whole story. It was too ugly, too complicated, and too personal.

"Well I got the investors to agree to remodel. Then we hired an agency that not only got us advertising in all the high-end, luxury magazines and blogs, but also got celebrities to stay with us. Once you get a few celebs, the rest flock to the hotel like flies, followed by the general public."

"That's cool. Maybe I should get some celebrity moms using my software app," she said

"Or celebrity dads." That made her laugh, which was awesome, because I got to see that off-kilter smile again. I was tempted to tell her how much I liked it. But I wanted to play it cool.

"Oh yeah. Dads change diapers, too." She held her hands up as if in surrender.

I might like her to surrender to me...

My phone buzzed. I grabbed for it and explained I needed to check in with my admin Trudy. Just like she'd done with her assistant.

Wait a minute. Was she beating me at my own game? Did she have her admin queued up to rescue *her*, in case I was a dud?

Nah. *I* was the shithead, not her. I texted Trudy back.

not ready to head out yet. give me 15

"So Nara, where are you from? Wait, my first question is, what kind of name is Nara?"

Damn, that smile was back. Crooked but wide with perfect straight teeth, and red lipstick. A real contrast to her pale skin.

"Nara is Irish for happy."

Nice.

She scooted closer to hear me. The restaurant was getting noisy with the dinner rush. Forty-five minutes had clearly come and gone. "And I'm from nowheresville, Indiana."

"I like that. Nowheresville." Boy, did she smell good.

"Yup. Got out of town on a college scholarship and never looked back."

"You still have family there? Friends?" I downed the last of my scotch. I was contemplating another, but once I got past two, I was committed to a night out. Possibly a very long night out. Maybe Miss Happy and her awesome smile would join me…

She shrugged. "Sort of. My mom is still there. My old friends are, too. I don't really keep up with them."

She looked down the length of the bar, clearly somewhere else for a moment. I didn't know where, but definitely not in a noisy restaurant in the busiest of American cities.

She continued, "My high school reunion is coming up. My mom's bugging me to go."

"And? Are you going?"

She shook her head. "Probably not. I mean, what am I going to do? Walk in there among all the people who never got to leave town and sit there and brag about having started a tech firm in New York City? I just don't think it's a good idea."

She was modest. I liked that.

"Okay. I can see that. If you don't want to go, you shouldn't."

She gazed directly at me and seemed relieved I agreed with her. It was clear the pressure to return home was all over her. I never understood why women got all riled up about things like that. Why didn't they just say *no* and be done with it? Seemed easy enough to me.

But then, I was an asshole.

She waved at the bartender for another round. Guess I wasn't going back to work.

"So what about you?" she asked. "Where'd you grow up?"

"Right here in New York City."

"No kidding! You have no accent," she said.

"I'll take that as a compliment. I went to boarding school in New Hampshire. That had a big impact on me," I said, barely listening to her.

Damn, her blue eyes were killing me.

"So when you were growing up, did you help out at the hotel?"

"I sure did. My dad made sure I learned to do everything from the time I was old enough to fold sheets and towels. I did every crappy job there was in that place."

I laughed, remembering how I'd hated that work then. But now I was damn glad he'd made me do it.

"Is your dad retired?"

That question was always a kick in the teeth. "Um, pretty much, yeah."

He was retired all right. At Sing Sing Correctional Facility, enjoying prison food. Dear old dad.

"That's cool. Do you see him much?" She finished her champagne or whatever it was she was drinking. And I'm pretty sure she sneaked a look at her watch.

"No, not really. I'm so busy with the hotel. It takes up a lot of my time."

Truth was I hadn't visited Dad since last Christmas.

And it was time to change the subject and fast. Her line of questioning was getting dangerously close to things I didn't like to talk about.

"So, Happy Nara, do you have time for some dinner tonight?"

This was one woman I wasn't going to let slip through my fingers.

But I don't think she was as happy about my invitation as I'd hoped. She slipped off her chair after throwing some money on the bar for the drinks.

"Gosh, Brodie, I actually have to get back to the office. You know how start-ups are. My workday doesn't usually end until nine or ten p.m."

She typed something into a text message

"Looks like my assistant Mimi is really needing me for something." She smiled and shrugged.

All right, if that's the way it was going to be…

I stood, too. Even in those sexy heels, she still had to look up at me. And god, I liked how she did that.

"It was a pleasure meeting you." She extended her hand, which seemed a little formal, but whatever.

"I'd like to see you again. I like your crooked smile."

Boom. I'd done it.

She looked nervous. Did I look like an axe murderer?

"Oh, thank you." She fumbled in her bag and produced a business card. "That would be nice."

I leaned in to kiss her cheek and inhaled the simple shampoo scent of her hair. Clean and beautiful, just like she was.

She gave another little laugh, and I realized her face had turned bright pink.

I'd embarrassed her. Now, if that wasn't the cutest thing.

Her phone buzzed again, and again she furiously responded to the text.

"Mimi again?" I had to torment her a little, especially since I knew she was beating me at my own game.

"Yes! Yes, something's going on at the office. I gotta go. See ya." And she went running out the door.

I watched her stride purposefully past the front of the restaurant window, never looking up from her phone. Good way to trip and fall.

Which I think I already had.

CHAPTER 9

NARA

The second I was back in the office, a blur of red hair rushed me.

"On my gosh! How was it? You stayed longer than I thought you would!" Mimi yapped, out of breath.

"God, girl, calm down. Were you on the edge of your chair the whole time I was gone?"

She trotted after me as I headed to my cubeand sat across from me once I'd settled in.

"So here's what you missed while you were gone." She ran down a list of all we had to do that night before we could call it quits.

I buried my head in my hands, ever so slightly buzzed by the alcohol.

"Don't worry," she chirped. "We'll get everything taken care of. When our beta test mommies come in tomorrow, they'll never know we were scrambling at the last moment in preparation for their kids' dirty diapers."

Just as she was wrapping up, Joi barged in, staring at Mimi until she took the hint and split.

With the chair vacant, Joi plopped down across from my desk and pulled her long, blond hair over her shoulder to twist the ends like she always did when she was about to be dramatic.

She plopped her feet up on my desk and took a deep breath. "These wedding preparations are killing me."

"I thought things were under control."

She threw her hands up and rolled her eyes. "My mom and Jack's mom are feuding over seating assignments. My shrink says weddings can bring out bad behavior in people, but I never expected this. I should have just handled everything myself, but I wanted to throw them a bone, make them feel important. Involved."

While she jabbered on about the wedding, I scrolled through my email. Damn, there was already one from Brodie.

He didn't waste any time. I flagged it for later.

"Nara? Nara? Hey, anybody home?" Joi asked, snapping her fingers.

I looked up from my laptop. "Oh, sorry. What were you asking?"

"I was asking if you picked up your bridesmaid dress yet."

"Oh, right. I had the final alterations done, so it's probably ready." I scribbled a note to call the shop tomorrow and returned to my email.

Joi went back to her wedding talk.

"Shit." I sighed. "Another email from Simon." My husband-not-husband.

"That asshole is still coming around?" she asked.

I peered around the wall of my cube to see who was in hearing distance. "Do you want to get some dinner in a half hour or so? I really want to talk but not here."

I felt a flash of guilt for not having gone to eat with Brodie. But what would be the point?

Joi, too, peeked around the corner at the office. At eight p.m., it was still full of people preparing for tomorrow. I was tight with my crew, but I was the boss, and they didn't need to know everything about my private life.

"I'll swing by in half an hour. You'd better be ready. No last minute emails or calls," she said.

I held my hands up in surrender. "Calm down. I'll be ready."

Twenty-five minutes later, Joi poked her head into my cube.

"I came early, knowing you'd need that much prodding to get out the door." She raised her eyebrows, waiting for my resistance.

And she was right. If she didn't drag me out the door, I'd never leave.

Sighing, I stuffed my laptop into my tote so I could do some work at home later, and on the way out told Mimi not to stay too late. She *would* stay late though, god love her, and everything would be ready for tomorrow.

Joi and I walked to Fettoosh, a Lebanese place not far from the office. In true New York fashion, diners were still streaming into the place even though it was nearly nine p.m. I hadn't eaten since my street vendor hotdog of about eight hours ago.

I ordered my usual *shish tawook* chicken kabobs, and she ordered the same thing she always did, which was something I could never pronounce. The owner brought us some nice, light Lebanese wine, and we got down to business.

"Okay," Joi said. "What did you want to talk about?"

"Okay. First of all, I met the guy I won at the Avenue A fundraiser auction thing. We had a drink just a few hours ago."

Her eyes widened. Already, she was missing the single girl life. Such as it was.

"Tell me…was he a total douche? You know those guys are always douches…" She was clearly hoping for a horror story.

I dug into the hummus the waiter had brought over.

"Honestly…he wasn't bad."

It kind of *was* disappointing that he wasn't a jerk. It was always fun to have a juicy bad date story.

Joi frowned. "Wait. What? They're always douches. Who else besides a conceited jackass would think they're hot enough to have people bid on them in public?"

"I know, right? But he was pretty cool, asked me some questions about myself, seemed smart and hardworking…"

She gave me her best exasperated look. I knew it well.

"Fine. But c'mon. You know what I'm interested in. What the hell did he look like? Spill it!" she demanded.

I hesitated to torment her further, and leaned forward conspiratorially.

"He was about the most freaking handsome guy I've ever seen up close and personal. Thick black hair, a little on the long side, square chin with a dimple in the middle, dark, dark eyes with lashes to kill for."

Joi's mouth fell open.

"And even in my heels, I had to look up at him." I demonstrated by craning my neck. "He must have been six-four."

She fell back in her chair. Maybe she shouldn't have been getting married after all.

"Wow. Well, you'll have to see him again. That's all there is to it."

She gave one of those "done deal" waves of her hand. Easy for her to say. She'd been with Jack since college and their getting married had been a foregone conclusion since then. She had no idea, really, how to date or what it was like.

"Yeah well, that's not gonna happen. I'm way too busy with the company." I looked around for the waiter. I was starving.

And I wanted to ignore the speech I knew she was about to give me.

"Oh, that's bullshit, and you know it. Everyone has time for a date now and then," she snapped.

Why were people who were in relationship always so pushy about making sure everyone else was paired off? It was as if being single was a disease.

"He did ask me to dinner, which I thought was very nice. But I came back to work instead."

The waiter finally came with my *shish tawook*. I grabbed my fork so fast I think I scared him.

Joi stared. "Are you crazy? Why the hell didn't you go?"

"Just didn't want to. I mean, I'm sure he's a jerk." I shrugged.

But on the other hand, I couldn't remember the last time I'd had sex. Maybe there *would* be a benefit to having won an auction date.

"But you just said…" She shook her head and picked up her fork, resigned to my stubbornness. We'd been friends so long she knew not to waste her breath.

I never did anything until I was damn good and ready.

She dropped it. "Okay, okay. I give up. So what else is going on?"

I had to tell her. It had been eating at me for days.

"You know Simon, right?" Of course she did. She tried to talk me out of marrying him way back when.

I should have listened.

"Ugh. Why aren't you divorced yet?"

She couldn't stand him, and had thought he was no good from the beginning.

But what could I say? I had been nearly broke, and ten grand had seemed like all the money in the world at the time.

"I *should* be divorced by now. But, he's turned out to be a major asshole." I sipped my wine.

I wasn't doing any more work today. Who was I kidding?

I continued. "He wants his ten grand back and is threatening to expose me if I don't pay him. And make the divorce difficult."

I set my fork down, my stomach soured at the thought of him.

"*What?* How can he do that? He'd just expose himself. He'd be deported."

She leaned toward me for emphasis. "He knows that, doesn't he? Or is he really that stupid? And how can he keep you from getting divorced?"

I nodded. "He has got to know that, and yet he's still trying to shake me down. He knows I won't let anything get in the way of the company's success. As for the divorce, I guess he could just make it really hard."

The color drained from her face, and she looked like she'd lost her appetite, too. I hated that she, the company, and our team could be affected by a bad decision I'd made years ago in a moment of desperation.

"Can you just pay him?" she asked quietly.

"That was my thought, too. Just get him the hell out of my hair. But one, I don't have an extra ten grand. I've sunk every penny I have into this business. You know that. And two"—I slapped my hand on the table, causing our wine to slosh—"why the hell should I? He got his citizenship. It was a fair exchange."

I shook my head. "I never should have broken the law. I'm paying for it now. I should have listened to you."

"Well, yes you should always listen to me. But you didn't," she said. "Why do you think he's coming after you now, instead of just getting the divorce underway?"

I shook my head. "He seems to think I'm making big bucks or something from the software app, which is really stupid. I thought everyone knew it took a long time for a start-up to make money. He refuses to believe I've maxed out my line of credit and that we're one mistake away from shutting our doors."

"Little does he know we're also one investor away from massive *success*," she offered.

And she was right.

But we'd been down that road many times, gotten our hopes up, only to have investors back out at the last minute for a variety of reasons—they might have found a better investment or had just plain changed their minds.

The first few times it had happened, I'd been devastated. I finally learned, however, it was just business.

If they didn't see the value in Mommy Knows, someone else eventually would.

But the fact that Simon was even *thinking* about undermining all that I'd worked for made me crazy with rage.

The waiter brought us some juicy, sticky *baklava* for dessert. But I could only play with mine, peeling off the thin layers of pastry until my plate was a thick mess of honey and ground pistachios.

Kind of how I viewed my life at that moment. A big, gooey mess.

CHAPTER 10

BRODIE

I'll be damned.

My auction date, Nara, had actually beaten me at my own game. I'd seen the text from her assistant when we'd been out for drinks, and it was clear the whole "emergency" thing was a set up. She'd needed an escape hatch in case I turned out to be a dud.

I can't blame someone for planning for the worst, but damn. A true first.

I'd fallen victim to my own trick.

On the way to work that morning, I got a call from Trudy. The band that had rented all the top floor penthouses had party number one underway—so named because they never left it at just one party—and there were naked girls running around the halls. They'd been up all night long.

I was normally inclined to let them do what they wanted to on their rented floors out of sight of other guests, but it seemed one of the girls had given a bellman delivering food a blowjob in front of an audience.

One of the maids had seen it and ratted him out.

Personally, I didn't care about the kid getting his dick sucked as long as everyone involved was a consenting adult. But when a party went beyond the confines of its rented space, I had to step in and make sure no one ended up naked in front of other guests, especially ones who were inclined to call the cops.

Sometimes, I was nothing more than a babysitter for rich, grown-up kids. But those overgrown brats spent a lot of money at my hotel, and they attracted people who spent even more.

Can't live with them. Can't live without them.

Accompanied by two of our beefiest hotel security men, I headed up to the penthouse to pay a visit to our latest rowdy guests.

After letting them know they needed to keep the party contained, everyone seemed happy. 'Course, the presence of the security guys helped keep negotiations friendly.

Hell, one of the guys from the band even offered me a line of coke. I didn't take it—I'm not into that stuff—but I took that as a sign of skillful diplomacy. Everybody won.

As I returned to my office, Trudy said, "Brodie, one of the front desk girls was just up here looking for you."

"What?" Needless to say, front desk staff did not spend much time in the management offices. "What did she want?"

Trudy raised an eyebrow and gave me one of those *I wasn't born yesterday* looks. Shit, did she know about the blowjobs?

"I don't know what she was doing up here, Brodie. And I don't think I want to know."

Busted.

"Yeah, well. We've flirted." If you want to call it that…

"Do you want to find out what she wants? I'll call her up here," she said, hands on hips.

Trudy was all about the no-nonsense.

"Yeah. Okay."

Not five minutes later, Sonya walked into my office. Damn, her hotel uniform looked good on her—snug enough to show off her great breasts, but tasteful enough for its purpose.

"Hi, Mr. Harcourt." She blushed. Poor thing was nervous.

Funny, she was all confidence when my dick was in her mouth.

"You can call me Brodie, like I told you. What can I do for you?" I smiled to put her at ease.

She looked down. I wasn't sure if the bashfulness was an act or the real thing.

She was shifting around on her feet, and she kept looking at me, then looking away. "Mr. Har—I mean Brodie, I was wondering if…I mean…you know, we could um, get together again?" She continued to avoid my gaze.

Her request was endearing. Seriously. And I considered it. I really did.

But I leaned forward, placing my elbows on the desk.

"Sonya, I enjoyed our playing. I did. You are a beautiful girl."

Now she was looking at me. "But I, um, am seeing someone. I'm sorry, sweetheart."

Shit. Did I really just say that?

An hour later, Trudy came in with my mail. "How'd your meeting go?"

"Huh? What meeting?" I asked, looking up from the reports I was reviewing.

"With the front desk girl."

There was an undeniable smirk on her face.

"She had a question." I took the stack of mail she'd opened. "Thanks for the mail, Trudy."

She rolled her eyes and shut the door as she left.

A strange invoice caught my attention. On close examination, I saw it was a bill for fifteen thousand dollars from a law firm I'd never heard of called Levin, Ross. It said:

Services rendered for dissolution of HWE Enterprises

What?

Dissolution of HWE…?

The partnership of Harcourt, Wooten, and Evershire…?

My business partners were dissolving our partnership…?

What. The. Fuck.

I dialed the number on the invoice.

"Levin, Ross. Pam speaking. You've reached accounting." A keyboard clicked in the background.

"Hello Pam. This is Brodie Harcourt from HWE Enterprises. I just received an invoice from your firm that I need some more information about."

More typing.

"Certainly, Mr. Harcourt. Let me pull up your account right now. HWE Enterprises did you say? Here we go. Looks like you met with one our attorneys from our business law practice, about…here it is, a month ago."

"Are you sure? Could you check?"

"Of course. Let me dig in deeper."

More clicking on the keyboard. "Oh, I see what happened here. The meeting was with Mr. Steven Evershire and Mr. Hardy Wooten. I see your name is here on the partnership documents. I guess that's why the invoice ended up with you. Should we have sent the bill to a different address, Mr. Harcourt?"

"No, not at all. I just, um, needed my memory jogged. Thank you for the info."

Unbelievable.

Steve and Hardy had engaged a law firm. Without me. About the dissolution of our partnership. The one I busted my ass for, day in and day out.

The one I built the best hotel in New York for.

No wonder they wouldn't talk to me about expanding to the West Coast.

They were trying to get rid of me.

I dialed my attorney, the one who'd represented me when everything went south with my father. His secretary knew me and sensed the urgency of my tone, and patched me right through.

"Brodie! Good to hear from you," my attorney said.

"Joe, I need to ask you something," I said.

"Sure, let me have it."

I took a deep breath and described the invoice and my call to Levin, Ross.

"Well. Sounds like you stumbled into some shit. Here's what it it looks like to me. If you each own thirty-three percent of the company, the other two owners can band together and either offer to buy you out or dissolve the company, and then immediately create a new one you are not part of. They can't take away your shares, but they can take away your job."

"Holy shit. Now that I've got the hotel on solid footing, the fuckers want me out," I said.

It was true, my dad screwed these guys over royally. I wasn't proud of it. But I'd been working my tail off to pay them back and then some.

"Brodie, do you want me to reach out to their attorney to see what's going on?" he asked.

"Not yet, Joe. Not yet. I'm gonna think on this for now. Figure out my next move."

He was silent for a moment. "All right, my friend. Keep me posted. And don't do anything without speaking to me first. Please."

CHAPTER 11

NARA

"Hey, Nara, can I come in?"

Without waiting for an answer, Michael, the company's accounting guy, invited himself into my cube.

"What's up?" I asked.

I'd been immersed in our software development schedule. Talking about money was about the last thing I was interested in at that moment.

Although seeing him made my heart speed up. Just a smidge. His close-cropped blond hair and beard made him cute but rugged. The kind of guy you want to take home to mom. And yeah, I'll admit it—we'd kissed before. And other things.

But that had been a while ago.

"I'm fine, Nara, thank you for asking," he snapped.

Oops. I held up my hands in a gesture of surrender.

"Sorry, Michael. I was in the middle of the dev schedule."

He leaned forward. "I wanted to go over the payroll with you. But first, I thought I'd tell you how hot you look today."

Oh, cripes.

"Michael." I stood and looked over the cubicle wall to ensure no one was close enough to have heard him.

"Not in the office, okay?"

As I sat back down, I realized his gaze was wandering all over me.

Was he really in here to talk about payroll? The folder on his lap just sat there, unopened.

"Hey." He lowered his voice, too. "When can we go out again?"

Okay. Now I knew what this was about.

"I don't know. I'm pretty busy, and you know Joi's wedding is coming up, and I'm the maid of honor."

Sure he and I had messed around a couple times in the past after a few too many drinks. But I didn't see myself dating someone like him and he probably didn't see himself dating me, either.

He just wanted to get his rocks off.

"Why don't we go to the wedding as dates?" he asked with a smarmy grin. He'd been invited just like everyone in the office had.

But I didn't need a date.

"Let's just meet there. I'll save you a dance, okay?"

His back stiffened, and he huffed a laugh. "You don't have to patronize me. You didn't seem to mind spending time together when I was licking your pussy, did you?"

"Jesus, Michael," I hissed. "Shut up!"

Mimi stuck her head around the corner of my cube

wall. "Oh, sorry. I didn't know you were in a meeting. I'll come back."

She turned to leave.

"Wait, Mimi. What's up?" Maybe she could help me get rid of him.

She glanced at her watch. "It's almost time for the dev meeting. Folks are gathering in the conference room."

"Right!" I popped up from my desk. "Was there anything else you needed, Michael? Could we finish the payroll stuff later?"

The asshole smirked. For god's sake. New York was full of women. Go find another.

Michael glared at me and filed out, followed by Mimi.

"Be there in a sec," I called after them.

I reached for my buzzing phone.

Well, I'll be darned. It was a text from Brodie.

you free for a drink?

Hmmm. I'd have to give that one some thought. I hustled to the conference room.

The development meeting went about as well as it always did, which meant not well at all.

The two lead developers—the guys who worked tirelessly to make the Mommy Knows app come to life in line with my vision for it—hated each other. I didn't know why. And I didn't care why.

All I wanted was for the app to be ready for the next round of beta-testing moms. We'd been experiencing some "false positives" where the app was notifying users of a dirty diaper when it was still clean.

That was bad. Really bad.

When I had filled out those high school aptitude tests, I never suspected I'd be thinking about pee and poop all day long.

I turned to look at my ringing phone. It was Simon. Lovely. I imagined for a sec blowing him off, but he was unpredictable, and I didn't want to mess with him. Especially while I was trying to get him to divorce me.

I ran back to my desk.

"Hello." I hated being civil to him.

"Nara, darling! How's my little wifey doing?"

"What's up, Simon?" There went the sour stomach churn.

He sucked in his breath. "You know what I'm calling about. Have you made any progress?"

"Simon, I think you might have a hearing problem. Or maybe it's a listening problem. So let me tell you again. I wasn't kidding when I said I didn't have ten grand."

An image of strangling him with my bare hands flashed through my thoughts. At least then I wouldn't have to divorce him.

"Stop fucking with me, Nara." His voice had lowered, transforming into something like a growl. I didn't know he had it in him. But I didn't know he had it in him to extort ten grand from me, either.

"I want my goddamn money, and I want it *now*."

Okay. I was done.

"Look, you little creep. You got your citizenship. You are entitled to nothing else."

"You're wrong there. Thanks to me and my investment in you, you've accomplished quite a lot. Like creating your own software firm. And I want a return on my investment."

"Simon?"

"Yes?"

"If you expose me, you'll be exposed, too. I will have to pay a steep fine. But you—you'll be deported."

He guffawed. "No, I won't darling. You know why?"

"Why?"

"Because they'll never catch me. I already have another identity to assume when the time is right."

His cold words gave me goosebumps. "Just like you, always figuring out a way to cheat the system."

"Hey, I wouldn't talk, my little friend. You are guilty of the same."

My hands fisted, and my back went rigid. "I broke the same law you did. But I will never, ever be the disgraceful scumbag you are."

I swiped my phone closed as best I could with a wildly shaking hand. I wasn't sure if my upset was from being pissed off, afraid, or both.

Nausea settled in my stomach. I had a feeling it'd be there for a while.

Heels clicking on the lobby's marble floor, I crossed to the huge doors leading from my office building to the hectic New York street scene.

"Good night, Miss Kincaid."

I waved at the front desk guard.

Just before I reached the doors, my phone vibrated. I considered ignoring it, which I almost never did. But curiosity got the better of me.

It was Brodie. Again.

hey. join me for a drink?

Hmmm.

i'm out front of your building.

Shit. Was I dealing with a stalker?

If he was in front of my building, it was too late to hide. I'd just exited the front doors. It was dark, but I was still under the building's lights. Most likely, he could see me—and I couldn't see him.

I looked around, checking out the pedestrians walking by and the cars parked at the curb. A limo window rolled down, and he leaned out. He looked terribly sexy with his open-collar dress shirt and suit jacket.

"Nara. Over here."

Why was I not surprised this guy traveled around in a limo?

Anyway, I guess I was committed. Maybe he'd be a welcome diversion from my crummy day. I hoisted my heavy tote over a shoulder and started toward the shiny black town car, conscious that he was watching my every step.

"This is a surprise," I said as he got out of the car and held the door for me. But I wasn't about to jump right in.

"Are we going somewhere?" I asked with a raised eyebrow.

He laughed and bowed as if I were royalty. "It's a beautiful evening. I thought I'd try to catch you on the way home from work. I remember your saying you leave between eight and nine every night, just like I do."

Oh, what the hell.

"Okay. Let's go." I slipped into the back seat of the car with a quick hello to the driver.

Brodie pulled the door closed behind us with a smooth *swoop*.

"Where we going?" I asked.

I had to admit, a drink sounded nice. And he sure was handsome, with that dark, brooding thing going on. So different from Michael at work. And the creepy Simon.

"What do you think about stopping by The Speakeasy in Brooklyn? That's where you live, right?"

Oh!

"I've always wanted to go there. To The Speakeasy, not Brooklyn."

He laughed at my lame joke.

"Cool, let's check it out." He leaned forward to give the driver directions.

I made a mistake with Michael at work. I'd made a colossal mistake with Simon.

I couldn't afford to make any more.

CHAPTER 12

BRODIE

I'd put myself out there for Nara, something I rarely did with women.

But my gut told me it would be worth it, and when she walked out of that office building, I knew I'd been right.

Luck must have been on my side, because she exited just as we pulled up in the limo. She'd stood outside the door, phone stuck in her face, reading what I figured was my text.

Under the overhang in the building's light, she struck a pose that about killed me. In her slim skirt and skyscraper heels, she was the definition of elegance.

What was different about her, though, was how she held herself—so unselfconscious.

She had a ridiculously large bag thrown over one shoulder. It must have been heavy as hell because she had to lean in the opposite direction to keep from toppling over. And while she wore those expensive, fuck-me style pumps, she was a little pigeon-toed. Not enough to look dopey, but enough to look like she wasn't trying too hard.

Her hair had been pulled back into some messy confection at the nape of her neck and from where I sat, it looked like strands were poking out all over. She looked *real*.

As she got closer, I rolled down the window and waved her over. I popped out of the limo, still not entirely sure she'd go anywhere with me. But there was no harm in asking, right?

She must have had a crap day like me, because she looked like she needed a drink, so we headed over to Brooklyn to a cool new place called The Speakeasy. Supposedly, it really *had* been a speakeasy back in the day.

"I should have known you ran around town in a limo," she said with a raised eyebrow.

"Yeah, well. I guess membership has its privileges." I laughed and shrugged.

Hey, I worked my ass off and made a good living. I deserved some of the convenience money could buy in New York.

Not to mention that having a pleasant way to get around town was the balls.

"So you never take the subway?" she asked.

Snarky. I liked that.

"Sure I do. You can't live here and not take the subway. But I grab the hotel limo whenever I can. It takes a lot of stress off the day."

She looked around, smoothing her hand over the leather seats. "Well, it sure is a nice treat. Hey, have you talked to *Page Six* yet? About our Avenue A auction date?"

I couldn't stand that useless gossip column.

"No. Not interested," I told her, shrugging.

She nodded. "I get that. I only spoke to them to get a little free publicity for my company."

Smart girl. "What'd you tell them?"

We hadn't spent much time together. Yet. What could she possibly have to say?

"Just that it was a lovely evening, and that maybe auction dating wasn't so bad." She laughed.

"Do you really feel that way?"

Now, it was her turn to shrug. "I wouldn't make a habit of it, but when it's for a good cause, why not?"

She reached up to gather some loose pieces of hair, and as she did, her blouse pulled out of her skirt. I spied a small amount of smooth, flat stomach, but it was the pierced belly button that caused my cock to twitch.

"I'm with ya on that," I agreed.

"You are?"

"I've been in a few of these auctions now, and the resulting dates are sometimes…shall we say, painful?"

That damn crooked smile of hers washed over me. "Tell me! I want to hear the dirt."

Not gonna happen. "Let's just say some of the folks I've met were not…people I'd usually spend time with."

She tilted her head, smart enough to read between the lines. "Okay. I get it. So you're saying you haven't picked up another auction girl after work, and offered them a ride in your big, bad limo?"

Wow. She made me laugh, something few people did. "I've never had a second date with someone I met through an auction."

Her eyebrows rose. "Oh. This is a date?"

"Jesus, you're a ball buster. Can we just have a nice time?" I asked with a wink. "Miss Happy?"

"You know, even though Nara means happy, I've never been called that."

"Do you like it?" I asked.

Nodding slowly, she said, "I don't know. It's kind of nice."

I leaned forward to knock on the window separating the driver from the back seat. "You can drop us here."

"Yes sir. Just give me a call when you're ready to return, Mr. Harcourt," the driver said.

I took Nara's hand as she climbed out of the car and held it until we reached the restaurant. In return, she gripped my fingers tightly, and it felt damn good.

The Speakeasy was gimmicky, but it was the perfect place to take a date.

We knocked on a nondescript front door—which was funny, because everyone knew it was the hottest new bar—and a tiny window opened as if we were sneaking into someplace forbidden. On the inside, the low lights and dark wood made for a cozy set up, and a waitress in 1920's-style gangster garb ushered us to a corner booth.

"This place is great," Nara said, flipping through the drink menu.

Up for trying the old Prohibition drinks, she ordered a highball and I got a sidecar.

"So what else did you tell *Page Six* about us?" I asked.

Having already read her brief interview, because I'm a spying bastard, I knew full well what she'd told them.

But I planned to have some fun putting her on the spot.

She blushed from light pink to almost purple and stirred her drink with the tiny straw it had been delivered with.

"Well. I told them auctions weren't my preferred way of meeting guys, and that you were nice enough, but that I didn't feel a spark."

She stared down at her drink.

"Well," I said. "There ya go."

I wasn't bothered in the least by her answer. What else was she going to say? That she wanted to marry me? I had to bite my tongue to keep from smiling.

She met my gaze. "I'm sorry, I didn't mean to insult you, or talk trash about you."

I popped a grin. There was no stopping it.

"Why are you smiling?" she asked.

I couldn't help it.

"I totally know what ran in *Page Six;* my admin showed it to me. I think it was hilarious."

She leaned back in her chair and relaxed. "So you asked just to embarrass me?"

"Pretty much," I said, nodding.

"Well, you got me on that. Cheers." She clinked her glass against mine. "In fact, they asked for a follow up in case we got together again."

"Jesus. Nosy fuckers, aren't they?"

She slapped my arm with a laugh.

"Well, I guess that's what *Page Six* is all about. However, the day after the article ran visits to our website shot up. I had no idea just how many people read that gossip column. Apparently, a lot of moms with kids in poopy diapers," she said.

"Hey, if you can make money off poopy diapers, I say go for it." I took her hand, pulling it to my lips for a kiss.

She stopped stirring her drink and looked at me for a tense moment. But she clasped my fingers right back.

With a slight smile, she continued. "The potential is there. We just need to perfect the app and get it to market."

I studied her. "Are you close?"

She pursed her lips.

"Yes and no. Sometimes the program sends the wrong message to the parents' phone. Not to get into too much gory detail, but the sensor that sits in the baby's diaper sometimes mixes things up. But we're getting there. Our last tests were really good. The moms we had come in loved it."

She looked at her watch. "We'd better pack it in. At least, I should. Got an early morning, and I still have work to do. The good news is that I can walk home from here."

Once out on the street, I realized I didn't want to let her go.

"You know, Nara, I wonder if there is a way I can help. With the company."

Surprise washed over her face. "Oh. Wow, thank you. But I don't see how you could."

"Do you plan to have a launch party or some other sort of event? You could do it at the hotel."

Her eyes widened "Really? I hadn't thought that far ahead."

"I have a lot of contacts. Not because I'm friends with

them, I just get a lot of business through the hotel. I wonder if I could hook you up with some celebrity mommies...?"

She shook her head in disbelief. "Oh my god. I should hire you to do my marketing. What an amazing idea. If they like the app, maybe they can give me their endorsement."

"Exactly." I laughed. "So much of the hotel business is about promotion. I think I've got it in my veins."

"That's nice of you to offer. I really appreciate it." She extended her hand for a shake.

Not quite what I was expecting.

So I took her hand and gently pulled her forward to place a kiss on her cheek. And damn if her hair didn't smell like pure heaven. And she turned, ever so slightly, toward my kiss.

That was all I needed.

I brushed my lips against hers, as I'd been dying to do since she got into the limo earlier. And to my delight, she returned the kiss with equal curiosity.

"Can I walk you home?" I offered.

She opened her mouth, but at first nothing came out.

In a breathy voice she managed, "Um...I'd like you to. I really would. But I think you'd better not. I'm just around the corner."

She was probably right. I wasn't sure I'd be able to leave her at the door. Especially when I saw how erect her nipples were.

"All right. Good night." This gave me another chance to kiss her, and this time I wasn't such a pussy. I pulled her from the waist and pressed my lips to hers, searching and exploring.

I wanted to know her, really know her, and thankfully, she fell into me like we were made for each other. When I pulled away because I didn't want to push too hard, she sighed, her eyes still closed.

I watched her walk down the street with her ridiculously heavy bag. I wished she'd let me walk her home, but I knew better than to push.

She seemed a little on the fence about me in spite of our hot kiss, and the last thing I wanted to do was give her a reason to run away screaming.

But if she was going to, I'd make sure she had a really good reason.

CHAPTER 13

NARA

What a pleasant surprise my impromptu date with Brodie had turned out to be. Not at all stalker-ish, even though he'd showed up at my office, unannounced, in his limo.

And then there were those kisses. God, he was hot.

But still…

Before I turned the corner toward my place, I looked back over my shoulder.

To my surprise, there he was, crouched, in conversation with a homeless man camped out on the sidewalk. He had a hand on the man's shoulder, and was nodding as they spoke. He reached for his wallet and pulled out some bills. Before leaving, he shook hands with him, leaving the man dazed by the uncommon act of kindness.

I slipped around the corner before Brodie saw me.

I'll be darned. I was dazed, too.

My heels were not the best things for walking on the old, uneven sidewalks of Brooklyn.

If I'd thought about it earlier, I would have switched to the flats in my bag. Never too late. I kicked off my heels before I broke my neck. Ahhh, my feet cried *thank you* as I slipped them into shoes that were actually good for my feet.

So Brodie had turned out to be quite charming, not to mention philanthropic. Although I still didn't know much about him—our drink had been a quick one. But it was generous of him to offer to help Mommy Knows. And I guess he really was committed to helping the homeless.

His involvement wasn't limited to showing up at fundraising auctions.

But his kiss…

My phone beeped. It was him texting me good night. I couldn't help but smile as I hurried home before my over-loaded computer bag permanently damaged my back.

It wasn't going to be easy to concentrate, that was for sure.

Next morning, I walked into Mommy Knows, and good old Mimi was already there. I headed back to my cube when Joi poked her head in.

"Hey girl," she yelled, half scaring me out of my wits.

"Jesus, Joi. Give me a heart attack, why don't you?"

She danced toward my desk. What the hell was she up to?

"I've got some gossip for you…" she sang.

Last thing I was in the mood for.

"I'm really not interested—"

She looked around gleefully. "Michael is fucking that temp receptionist we have up front."

Ooof.

Had someone punched me in the gut? Because it felt like it. I didn't even like Michael, and though we'd messed around, we were certainly not in any sort of relationship. And I'd rebuffed him only recently.

So then why did I feel like a chump?

I'd been in high school when I'd gone through my slut stage. Although it was more like a slut on steroids stage. When I'd emerged from it—bad reputation and all—I had a newfound commitment to academics and to getting the hell out of Dodge. But while in the middle of it, I jumped from guy to guy, desperate for approval and some sort of teenage connection.

But the boys had always moved on to another girl by the next time I saw them in the school hallway.

And Mom wondered why I never wanted to come back home?

"Joi, I could give a shit who that guy sleeps with. It's his business. As long as he keeps doing his job."

She rolled her eyes. "Touchy. I'll come by later when you're not in such a shitty mood."

"Joi—" But she was gone.

My phone vibrated. *Shit.*

"Hi, Simon," I said with all the enthusiasm I could muster.

They say you get more bees with honey…and it was too early for drama, anyway.

"Darling! I saw your story in *Page Six*," he said with glee. "I'm sorry your dating life has become so ho-hum."

"Simon, what do you want?"

"Oh, just to say hello to my favorite wife. Well, my only wife. And to see how your fundraising efforts have been going. You know, perhaps you could hold another one of those date auctions. They seem like good moneymakers."

I lowered my voice and whispered, "Simon, go fuck yourself."

Oh, that felt good.

"Oh, sweetie. If you're smart—and I *know* you are—you wouldn't go 'round pissing me off."

"I don't have your money. I've told you that. But if I did, I still wouldn't give it to you. I earned that money by marrying you, which I have really come to regret," I hissed.

"Well, you'll have many more regrets in your future if you don't come to your senses."

Something snapped. I was done. Just done.

"Look. Don't call me anymore. Not ever again unless you are bringing me divorce papers. Otherwise, stay away from me or I'll get a restraining order."

He laughed. "You can't get a restraining order against me. I've never touched you, and I pose no physical danger to you at all."

"Don't worry. I can embellish a story as well as the next person. And I'll do that if I need to. So like I said, stop calling me. Or *you'll* be sorry."

"Now, Nara, I would be careful if I were you—"

Shaking, I swiped my phone closed and buried my face in my hands.

The phone buzzed again. Brodie.

had fun last night. let's do it again.

Ugh. All these men could go to *hell.*

At lunchtime, Joi and I called an Uber to run over to the bridal shop for her last fitting. With the wedding two weeks away, the pressure was on, and she spent the better part of each day on the phone with caterers, florists, calligraphers, and a dozen other vendors who were playing a part in her big day.

And then there were the families.

I vowed to remain single. I had no interest in the bullshit drama Joi was going through, and besides, my company took all my time and energy. I'd be damned if I was going to waste that on some guy who would only let me down in the long run.

But that wasn't to say I was not up for some fun...

"We're here!" Joi squealed, practically jumping out of the Uber before it fully stopped. She ran for the bridal shop's front door like she was greeting an old friend, leaving me behind to approach it with my usual scorn.

After all, I was several hundred bucks into this wedding thanks to this place.

Stop.

I had to buck the bad attitude, if not for Joi's sake, then for mine. I didn't have the spare energy to walk around with a chip on my shoulder. Her special day was coming up, and she deserved to be celebrated by someone who wasn't wearing a resting bitch face.

I sat on one of the salon's white, fluffy sofas and nibbled on Jordan almonds. My dress was ready, waiting for me to pay the balance at the front desk. Oh, there was nothing I wanted to do more than spend four hundred dollars on a dress I didn't even like.

But hey, what were friends for?

Joi bounded out of the dressing room in her partially fitted gown, the back wide open, holding fluffy layers of tulle and other fabric.

"Well?" she said, twirling in front of me.

I had to admit, she made a pretty bride.

"They're going to have me come in for one last fitting just a few days before the wedding, because I'm still losing weight. Can you believe it?" She skipped back to the dressing room with the saleslady running after her.

My phone buzzed. Brodie again.

i have an offer you can't refuse. well, shouldn't refuse

That made me laugh. And damn if I didn't need a laugh just then. Even though I wanted nothing to do with dating.

if I can't refuse it, do I get to know what it is?

Oh my god. Was I flirting?

nope.

Well, then.

what if I don't trust you?

you would be smart. miss happy

Oh what the hell. The memory of him helping the homeless guy melted my cold heart.

you still there? he asked.

yes, sorry. at a bridal salon

you getting married ?

um, no. my friend is

whew. i'm not into married women

Note to self—don't let this guy know I actually *was* married. Married to an asshole in a fake union, but married nonetheless. I continued the text-versation.

what kind of women are *you into?*

Joi came bounding out of the dressing room again, saleslady in tow.

"What do you think of this headpiece? I might get it instead of a veil." She was breathless in her excitement. Bridal salons were her kryptonite. What she would do for fun after the wedding was over, I had no idea.

"Mmmm. I like the veil better." Actually, I hated veils, but I knew Joi loved them. Her indecision was just last minute jitters.

She ran back into the dressing room with that poor woman on her heels.

I returned to my phone. Shit, had I really just asked Brodie what kind of women he liked? But before I could make a joke about it, his answer popped into my phone.

women like you

So. There it was. My heart pounded, because the ball was in my court. Well, my virtual court. He liked me. He was handsome and sexy.

What the hell was *wrong* with me?

But I needn't have worried. Before I was able to come up with something clever to say, he let me off the hook.

so what do you say to my offer you shouldn't refuse?

what's the offer?
a date. with me
that's all you'll tell me?
that's all you need
well then. okay. i accept

CHAPTER 14

BRODIE

Damn if that Nara wasn't one tough customer.

If I hadn't been unable to stop thinking about her gorgeous face, long legs, brains, and smart-ass attitude, I might have thrown in the towel by then.

What was it about her? I mean, she was beautiful and classy, sure. Ambitious, too. And she didn't give a shit about my money. But what really got to me was that she was making me *work* for it.

And that was something new.

I was trying to head out of work early on a Friday afternoon, unusual for me.

Weekends were the cash cows of the hotel business, and I'd normally be busting my ass, making sure everything was in place for the next three days of craziness. Not that we weren't busy during the week, it's just that things were calmer...and slower. Weekday guests were normally here for business.

But weekend guests were here for pleasure, and they had an entirely different set of expectations. Everything had to be fucking perfect.

And it nearly always was.

I hadn't been in touch with my conniving business partners since I'd found out about their plan to screw me over. I was still thinking through the best way to handle things. But my ass was chapped that those fuckers even thought for one moment they could take away the hotel my dad built from the ground up.

"Dalt," I said, calling my brother in Sausalito.

"Yo, Bro. What's up?"

I heard seagulls in the background. Living the California life. Fucker.

"Dude. I got a story for you. Do you have some time?"

"Sure. I just finished cleaning my brushes."

I pictured him taking a seat on the old beat up couch in his studio, bright sunlight shining everywhere, a nice ocean breeze blowing through…

I sat. "So, I got this weird piece of mail last week."

I shared the whole story of how I'd accidentally discovered my business partners' meeting with a law firm to discuss breaking up the HWE partnership.

"Holy shit," he said. "Can they even do that?"

"It looks like they can." I shared with him the conversation I'd had with my attorney Joe. Talking about it left me with a grinding burn in the pit of my stomach. I hadn't experienced anything like it since my dad's trial.

"So what are you gonna do?" he asked.

I sucked in my breath. "Dunno yet. I'm trying to think

it through calmly. Maybe find a way to surprise *them*. I have a few ideas brewing."

"Okay. I'll get you in touch with those new investors soon. That should open up some options," he said.

"Thanks, Dalt. I know I can always count on your support."

"We'll figure it out," he said.

He was right.

On my way through the hotel lobby, the receptionist, Sonya, eyed me.

Since I'd rebuffed her, she'd mostly ignored me, but in an effort to keep her from feeling uncomfortable, I'd gone out of my way to be friendly. I walked over to her after she helped the last guest in line. Scott, the other staff member on the desk, nodded and went back to his work.

"Sonya, how has your day been?"

She looked surprised. Still pissed, perhaps.

"Very good, Mr. Harcourt. And yours?" She smiled, but there was something hard behind her eyes. Had she thought something would come of our little encounters?

I was a freaking idiot. Would I ever learn?

I leaned toward her and said in a lowered voice, "I hope you've been well. Again, I'm sorry we couldn't continue what we started. I'm really sorry."

And I was. Sort of.

I must have said something right, because I could swear her expression brightened. I looked over to see

Scott watching us, but he quickly put his nose back in his computer and out of our business.

Sonya looked around and sneaked a finger across the front desk to touch my hand. "It's okay, Mr. Harcourt. I knew it had to end some time."

"I appreciate your understanding, Sonya. And I appreciate all your hard work."

"You're welcome." She was smiling now but also looking over my shoulder. New guests were coming in. Perfect timing.

"Talk to you later," I said.

"Yes, Mr. Harcourt. Of course."

I had the limo run uptown to pick up Nara, who had no idea where we were going.

The driver let me know he'd returned with her, so I could head out front to jump in.

"Hey, gorgeous," I said, pulling the car door shut behind me.

And boy, did she look gorgeous. Hair pulled up into a neat ponytail, loose black trousers, and what looked like another of her signature white blouses. It didn't get much classier than that. And of course, she was dragging around her bag loaded with bricks.

I planted a hot one on her delicious lips.

"Brodie! Fancy meeting you here." She laughed.

"Okay, so now Miss Happy is a joker?"

The late afternoon sun shone in the car window and

illuminated her flawless skin. She reached over and clasped my fingers.

"Just keeping you on your toes, Mr. Hotel Guy." She turned to fully face me. "Now are you going to tell me where we're going?"

I looked out the window and realized we were nearly there. I nodded toward a sign.

Her brows wrinkled. "What are we doing at a heliport?"

"What do you think, Happy? We're going for a helicopter ride."

"No way! I've never been in a helicopter."

"Well, you're gonna love it."

Her brows knit together. "I don't know. Where are we going?"

"We're flying over Manhattan and then to the Hamptons for dinner."

Her mouth dropped open just as I'd hoped it would. "No way! I have to get to work in the morning. Even though it's Saturday, I have a load of things to do."

I wrapped an arm around her and pulled her to me. "Don't worry. We'll be in Montauk in forty minutes. We'll have dinner and head back home. In fact, I bet I'll have you back home before nine thirty since we're off to such an early start."

I opened the door and held out my hand.

"Are you coming? Or do I have to have dinner by myself?"

We were finally thirteen hundred feet in the air, both struck speechless. I'd flown over Manhattan many times, but never failed to be dumbstruck by the view from above.

Aside from the bright yellow taxis, the typical noise, movement, and crush of people were invisible from this high up. It all looked so damn peaceful. Which of course was a total illusion.

"Oh my god, there's the Chrysler Building!"

I leaned forward to tap the pilot on the shoulder and made a *spinaround* motion with my finger. He knew exactly what I wanted, and got as close as he could to the building to circle it.

"Holy shit. I can see people in their offices!" She pressed her hands against the windows like a little kid.

It amazed me, too.

To see the most powerful city on Earth, where it looked about as intimidating as a sleeping baby, was just plain difficult to grasp. Her hand reached for mine as she leaned across me to the other side of the helicopter.

"Are you scared?" I asked.

She thought for a sec and shook her head. "No. Not at all. It's so peaceful. I'm just blown away. I'll never have the same perspective on New York again."

That was exactly how I felt.

We finished our tour of the spit of land that was Manhattan and headed east, flying over the bedroom communities of Long Island.

Nara's fingers gripped mine tighter when a burst of wind bounced us around, and I lifted her hand to my lips. She looked at me, quietly settling back into her seat.

"Look at the beaches," Nara said. They were long and sweeping, and we were low enough to see the tide coming in.

"It's so magical," she added.

We landed a few minutes later and a cab took to dinner at Flagstone, one of the best restaurants in the small Hamptons beach town of Montauk.

Before we entered the restaurant, I turned and saw her looking at me with those blue eyes.

I took my best shot and lowered my mouth to hers.

NARA

What a freaking awesome diversion from, well, everything.

Brodie first dazzled me with a helicopter ride (a helicopter ride!) over Manhattan, and then dinner in the Hamptons.

I mean, who the hell lived like that?

I'd met some wealthy people during my time in New York. The city was full of them. But I'd never known someone who lived at this level of luxury. I mean, the guy obviously worked his butt off. It didn't seem as if anyone gave him his good fortune from what I could see.

But what did I know? Truth was, I knew hardly anything about him aside from the fact that he ran a successful New York City hotel. And participated in silly bachelor auctions.

When his driver picked me up at the office, minus Brodie, I thought, what the hell? Why'd he ask me on a date and then not even pick me up himself? But we swung by the hotel to get him, and headed over to the Wall Street Heliport, usually reserved for the city's titans of finance and industry.

Who knew that crazy Manhattan, and boring suburban Long Island, could be so beautiful from up in the air? And then we landed in Montauk, on the far eastern end of the skinny peninsula that was the Hamptons, the collection of seaside communities for New York's well-off.

I could get used to living like this. But I wasn't going to.

Even if the guy did kiss like a champ.

We settled into our table at Flagstone, a restaurant I'd only ever heard about. Of course, it was elegance personified—white table linens, fine silver, lots of glistening crystal on every table, and incredible views of the water. A glass of bubbly seemed kind of uninspired, so I went all out and ordered a martini.

"So, Mr. Brodie. I barely know anything about you. Educate me."

I chomped on one of the most beautiful breadsticks I'd ever seen. Delicious, too.

He sipped his scotch and sat back in his chair, enjoying the view of the Atlantic Ocean. If it was possible, he was even more handsome in profile, with that square chin and his crazy thick eyelashes. "Well, Miss Happy. I'm boring. I'd rather hear about you."

"Okay, then. What would you like to know?"

"All right," he said. "Tell me the best thing that happened to you today and the worst thing."

I shrugged and took the tiniest sip of my martini.

"I'm boring," I said, shrugging. "Nothing to report."

Except I was being extorted by a crazy Englishman, my business was on the rocks, and I was being hounded to attend a class reunion I'd rather die than attend.

"C'mon. Spill it. I know you have something to tell me about your day. I can see it on your face."

Christ. Was he a mind reader? Well fine. If he wanted to hear my shit, then my shit he would hear. I leaned onto the table so I could lower my voice and looked around conspiratorially.

"Well. My husband called me at work to harass me for ten thousand dollars. Other than that, the day was fairly routine."

I figured that would be the end of that. Check please! Catch the helicopter back to the city, and never hear from the guy again.

But he rolled with it. Gotta give him credit.

"Really? That sucks," he said. "My wife called today to tell me she was pregnant with our tenth child. And I had a vasectomy three years ago."

I tried looking at him seriously but burst out laughing.

"That was the best comeback ever," I said, trying to catch my breath. "I gotta hand it to you."

He blew on the back of his knuckles and rubbed them on his chest. "What can I say?"

Then he sucked an oyster from its shell.

Why did I find that so sexy?

"So. Did your husband really call you today?" he asked.

Might as well spill it.

"Yup," I said, slurping my own oyster.

"Damn. Miss Happy is a married woman. I'm not usually into married women." He sipped his scotch and downed another oyster.

I kept drinking and slurping, hoping that was the end of that conversation. Why I'd brought it up, I didn't know.

The waiter dropped off our lobster roll sliders, some of the cutest little edibles I'd ever seen. We both dove in, lost in the exquisiteness of fresh seafood.

After a few minutes, Brodie asked, "So. Is there anything you want to tell me?"

"No." I took another sip of my martini. It was a small sip.

"You sure? He looked at me with a raised eyebrow. "Are you married or not?"

I set my seafood fork down and dabbed my mouth with the corner of my napkin.

"I actually am married," I told him.

"Ah ha. So you weren't kidding." So far, he seemed unfazed.

"When I was just starting my business, I took money from an English guy to marry him so he could get his green card."

He nodded. He was being cool so far, so I continued.

"In the end, it was a mistake."

He finished his chewing and asked, "How so?"

Big sigh. "Contrary to our agreement, he now won't give me a divorce, and he wants his ten thousand dollars back. I don't have the money, and he's threatening to tell my investors. That would ruin my company."

A rush of emotions suddenly overwhelmed me. A lump built in my throat and my eyes filled with tears. Great, crying on a date. Good going, Nara. But it felt good to tell him.

If this didn't scare him off, I didn't know what would.

"Jesus," Brodie said. "What a fucking dick."

It was as if his sympathetic understanding broke a hole in the dike holding my emotions, because out of the blue I found myself sobbing quietly. I blew my nose into the high-end linen napkin on my lap.

"I'm so sorry," I said between hiccups. "I didn't mean to get emotional on you. It's just that this has really been weighing on me. I'm a wreck over it."

"Christ, I don't blame you. What a shitty thing to go through."

I nodded. "Yup. Karma, I guess. That's what I get for breaking the law."

"What a story."

The waiter dropped off our dinner, and seeing my face, disappeared just as quickly.

"You're not kidding," I said, wiping away the last of my tears with the back of my hand.

"What are you gonna do about it?" he asked.

I thought for a sec.

"I'm not really sure yet. On one hand if he exposes me, it could be the end of my company. But on the other, *he* would be deported. Although he seems to have figured that out. He's ready to hide under a fake identity."

He shook his head in disgust. "This guy sounds like more of a loser every minute."

"Yup. And I married him."

I arched my neck and rolled my shoulders. It felt damn good to have gotten that off my back.

"Now, you tell me something," I said, although it was doubtful he had anything half as dramatic as I did.

He sliced into his filet mignon. "A couple years ago, my father was convicted of fraud and embezzlement. He's in prison now."

He popped a bite of steak into his mouth.

Holy shit. Now *that* was a story.

"Damn," was all I could say. That was why dad was no longer in the hotel business. Okay.

"Yup. That's what I said when I found out."

"Where is he in prison?" I asked.

"Oh, not far from here. Sing Sing Correctional Facility in Ossining. About an hour north of the city."

"Wow," I said. "I'm sorry to hear that."

"Let me tell, you, so was I."

CHAPTER 16

BRODIE

Christ, I couldn't believe I told her my dad was in prison. Was I fucking crazy? I never told anyone that willingly.

"How did it all go down?" she asked.

"My dad's business partners found out he was shifting money around to get them through a rough patch. He could have handled it differently—it's not like he was hurting for money. But they took the case to the DA, and he ended up in prison."

She took a bite of her halibut. "How'd you end up in charge of the hotel?"

"Well, the agreement we worked out was that I would run the hotel and make payments to the plaintiffs—in this case, my dad's business partners. They eventually passed away, and now, I'm dealing with their sons. We had to put together a partnership, and I've done well by them. I want to make it up to them."

"That is a lot to take on, especially when you didn't even wrong those folks."

"Yeah. Well, I love the hotel. My dad built it, and I practically grew up there. This arrangement was really the only way to save it."

"I'm impressed. You're making it work," she said.

"Well, it's not been without its issues. In fact, I'm afraid something serious is brewing right now."

God, it felt good to talk about this.

"What's going on?"

I told her the story of my call to the firm and how the dissolution of the partnership might work.

"Oh my god! What are you going to do?" she asked.

I took a sip of the Opus One wine I'd ordered. Sublime…like the stunner sitting across from me.

"I'm not sure, yet. I'm thinking through my options."

"Wow, just wow. And I thought I had problems." She gave a small laugh and shook her head.

I held my glass to her.

"Cheers. May all our problems be solved. Eventually."

I thought I'd been smitten by women before, but apparently, I'd fooled myself. This here, this was the real thing.

Nara was a scrapper, not some spoiled Manhattanite like I was used to. When she excused herself for the ladies' room, all I could do was stare at the lipstick on the rim of her martini glass.

Get a grip, asshole.

After dinner, we had time to kill before the helicopter

returned to pick us up. We headed toward the moonlit beach where a light breeze was blowing off the Atlantic.

Much to my delight, she shivered, giving me another excuse to wrap my arm around her. Funny, I never needed an excuse to touch a woman before. But with Nara, I wouldn't make assumptions.

Patience was suddenly a valued virtue.

We headed toward a pier where a couple old guys were fishing. We passed them, and at the end of the old wooden structure, we leaned on the railing and looked down at the black water circling around barnacled pilings. I inhaled the saltwater smells, which reminded me of coming here as a kid.

My family hadn't taken helicopters to get here back then. We'd piled into an old Volvo station wagon back before my dad had made it big with the hotel. Back before he'd screwed up badly enough to end up in prison.

I turned to find Nara, eyes closed, face turned into the breeze. A few strands of her inky hair had come loose and whipped around her face. Goddamn if she didn't take my breath away.

I ran a light finger from her temple to her cheek, and I tucked the errant hairs behind her ear. Her eyes remained closed, but her lips formed a slight smile. She sighed deeply.

I brushed my lips over hers, and she released the hottest little moan. In seconds, my dick was standing at attention inside my trousers.

I ran the tip of my tongue over her relaxed lips. They parted with my gentle probing. She tasted like wine, only sweeter, and it was all I could do to keep from devouring her.

When I pulled her closer, her hands fell on the back of my own neck, running through my hair. She grabbed a handful and hung on hard.

Playing rough. I did not expect that.

Pulling back, I left her needing more. I had a sudden urge to see her face, which was all the more beautiful in the dark where I could really only see the contrast of her blowing hair against her fair skin. I cupped her cheeks.

"You're something, Miss Happy."

She looked down, maybe in embarrassment, I wasn't sure. Then her gaze met mine.

"You're not too bad yourself, Hotel Guy."

"You know what?" I asked.

"What?"

"The cab is here to take us back to the helicopter." I laughed.

I could swear she looked a little disappointed that our intimate moment had to end. But she needn't worry. There'd be more.

The flight back to the city was more amazing than the flight east to Montauk, with the lights of Long Island and then Manhattan glittering below.

It was a quiet ride back, mesmerized as we were and buzzed thanks to good dinner wine. The limo met us at the heliport and immediately steered toward Brooklyn to take Nara home. Our evening would be over in fifteen or so quick minutes.

Unless I could find a way to prolong it.

I held her hand in my lap, making circles on her palm with my finger as she scooted closer and put her head on my shoulder.

"Well, would you look at that," I said. "Just barely nine thirty. Did I tell you we'd get you home at a decent hour or what?"

She glanced at her watch. "You weren't kidding. Wow."

We pulled up in front of her place.

"Walk me to my door?" she asked.

We climbed the stoop to a brownstone that had probably been a single family home back in the day. Now, as a sign of the times, the placed had been divided into what looked like four units, two on each level. Regardless, it was beautiful, and the dark wood entry way was infinitely cozy and warm.

It made me rethink my spartan Soho loft.

"Gorgeous building."

"Want to take a quick peek?" she offered.

"Sure I won't be keeping you up past your bedtime?"

She laughed. "I may keep you up past *your* bedtime."

Damn.

We entered her apartment, and before she could flick on a light, I pressed her against the foyer wall and ground my lips against hers. I'd been waiting all night to do this, to really take her, and I hoped she was as open to it as I wanted her to be. She grabbed my shoulders and pulled me tighter still.

My dick was rock hard, and I ground it against her stomach. She pressed right back into me. Shit.

I gave us enough separation that I could reach the buttons of her silk blouse. The second I got it open I pulled one of her juicy tits out of her lace bra and brought it to my lips. Her nipple was tight and pointed in my mouth, and I sucked on it until she moaned and ground my head harder into her chest.

I wanted to take her and fuck her right there.

But I knew better. If I wanted this woman, I had to ease into her life. There was something in her past holding her back. I wanted to find out what it was and annihilate it.

Unless she annihilated me first.

CHAPTER 17

NARA

I had to hand it to him...Brodie had far more self control than I gave him credit for.

I mean, he'd pressed into my stomach what seemed like a very nice erection, and just when I thought I would faint from him torturing my nipple, he pulled back as if it were time to go home.

Not so fast.

Not sure what came over me, but I wanted to make him feel good. No, I wanted to make him feel great. And I guess I wanted to prove to myself that I could do it. I reached for his trousers and as fast as my fingers would allow, unbuckling, unbuttoning, and unzipping until I reached him.

And what a treasure I discovered.

He was hard as a baseball bat, and when I freed him from the tangle of shirttails and boxers, his cock bounced in freedom. I ran my hand along the shaft, which was too wide to completely close my fingers around, and marveled at the velvety softness of his skin.

When I reached the head and stroked a little more gently, I could swear he growled.

"Nara. Fuck, that feels nice."

That was all the encouragement I needed. I fell to my knees and pointed him in the direction of my lips.

First, I licked a drop of precum from him, and then tormented him with circles around his crown. Then I took his whole head into my mouth—only the head—and created a suction that hollowed my cheeks. He looked down at me, his hands on my head. His balls were already pulled up nice and tight.

I pulled his cock out of my mouth, and ran it over my cheek, dying to feel him all I could.

I encircled his head once more with my lips, sucking and licking the most sensitive part, while he stroked the length. Little by little I took more of him until my lips replaced his hand, and he banged into the back of my throat.

My knees were getting sore from the hardwood floors, but truthfully, I barely felt them. My own sex was wet and hot, and more than a little achy.

I was pistoning his cock with my mouth in a steady rhythm when he pulled away from me and pulled me up by the arms. I barely knew what was happening, so engrossed I was in sucking him off, and before I knew it I stood there in nothing but my panties and high heels.

I went to kick off the shoes.

"No. Keep them on."

He threw off his own shoes in order to step out of his

trousers, and when he did, he picked them up to fish something out of his pocket. He ripped open a condom and handed it to me.

"C'mere," he said, leading me into the living room. He pushed me against the sofa.

"Put the condom on me, please," he said quietly.

I rolled the tight latex over his engorged hard-on, and as soon as I was done, he spun me around and bent me over the sofa back. He yanked my panties over my ass and down to my knees and his fingers flew to my hungry pussy.

It had been so long for me—too long, really—since I'd been lightheaded from the touch of a gorgeous, confident man. I'd missed it more than I'd realized.

"Are you ready, beautiful?" he asked.

"Yes," I murmured.

He kicked my feet farther apart, and I felt him press up against my slit while I impatiently waited for him to stretch my pussy wide.

He entered just enough to open me, leaving me gasping.

"You all right?" he whispered.

"More," I murmured.

And he did give me more, sinking deeper inside, an inch at a time so I could accommodate his girth. One last push, and his balls bounced against my clit.

He was seated in me to the hilt, holding himself there, while my orgasm built. I hadn't known I could come that way, but my pussy contracted until I exploded over his thick hardness, while I was bucking my head and calling his name.

Just as I began to quiet, he began to pump again, plunging in and out of me until another orgasm built and I was bucking and screaming all over again. I couldn't see or think, or even speak.

All I could do was mindlessly feel him, and the resulting, delicious sensations exploding over me.

In my delirium I only partially realized Brodie swelling inside me, and then convulsing into shudders.

"Yeah, it's so good. Baby, it's so good," he murmured as his pumping slowed.

He pulled out of me, discarded the condom, and pulled us down to lie on the sofa where we dozed.

When I woke, Brodie had pulled a throw over me and was dressing.

"Where are you going? What time is it?" I asked, sitting up, groggy.

"Around eleven p.m. You have a big day tomorrow, and I do too. I'm gonna head home. And I'll call you later."

He sat down next to me on the sofa, smoothing the mess that was my hair away from my face. No one had ever looked at me like that—as if he knew me, and could really *see* me—but also with an intense curiosity, as if he wanted to know more.

As the door closed behind him, I lay there on the sofa where he'd left me, disheveled as hell with lipstick smeared down my chin, my ponytail decimated, and a warm ache in my pussy.

But I came to my senses and ran to the front window to spy on him as he climbed into a cab; he must have sent the limo driver home long ago. He cut quite a figure with his height and broad shoulders in his perfectly fitted dark suit. I felt a little pang watching him pull the door closed.

But just as he pulled away, he rolled down his window and took a last look at my place.

I wondered if he saw me, because a text came in moments later.

g'night beautiful. c u soon.

I didn't answer. I wanted to play it cool. I'd thrown myself on enough men with disastrous consequences and didn't want to humiliate myself again.

I slept like the dead, and when my phone rang at midnight, it scared the wits out of me.

"Hello? Hello?" I croaked. I reached for the glass of water I kept on my bedside, but in my clumsy sleepiness sent it flying to the floor. I struggled to sit up and wipe off the nightstand before I had the presence of mind to wonder who the hell was calling so late.

"Nara? Nara is that you?" I wasn't awake enough yet to identify the caller, but it was an accent from my past.

"Yes, this is Nara. Who's this? Did something happen to my mother?"

"Nara, calm down! It's Becca Kates."

Becca Kates? High school Becca Kates?

"Becca, why are you calling me so late? It's midnight here."

"Oh my goodness. I forgot about the time change. I'm so sorry! I always do that to you, don't I? Listen, how 'bout I call you back tomorrow?" she offered.

"No, it's okay. I'm awake now."

Did I hear a baby crying in the background? "Becca, is that a baby? I thought your kids were older now."

She laughed.

"You're right. The older ones are, well, older. I had another baby since we last spoke, sweetheart! In fact, I just got him down, and now he's crying again. Bill!" she screamed into the phone. "Honey, go get the baby."

All the commotion made my ovaries shrivel.

"Nara, I'll get right to the point since I'm calling you so late."

"Okay."

"Are you comin' home for the reunion or not?"

Oh shit. The damn reunion.

But before I could come up with another excuse—I'd already used several—she continued.

"Now look, I know you have to come a long way. But you can stay with me and Bill and the kids if you don't want to stay at your mom's house," she offered.

The dread that came with even considering attending the reunion left me in goose bumps.

"Gosh Becca. I'm not sure I'll be able to come back for that."

"What? You're kidding, right? *Everyone's* gonna be there. It'll be the party of the year!" she insisted.

Was she kidding, asking me if *I* was kidding?

Of course not. Because for her, it *would* be the party of the year.

The old guilt had been building, and now, it lodged somewhere in my gut, like a huge ball of something toxic.

Could I actually tell her I didn't want to go without insulting her?

But she was more than oblivious to my apprehensions. I mean, how could I go back there and tell everyone about my new life as a CEO and entrepreneur in New York City? For one, they'd look at me like I had three heads. And second, I was afraid of rubbing it in their faces—I'd gotten out, and they didn't.

Then, there were the fuckers I'd slept with. Thank god I hadn't gotten pregnant. I might never have escaped.

"Becca, can I let you know later whether I'm coming? And if I can't make it, I promise to come home another time. I'd like to see you and Bill. And the kids."

"All right, sweetie. But let me know soon. I know these tickets are gonna sell out, and I want to make sure we have one for you. I'm head of the committee again in case you didn't know," she said.

The crying started up again. I guess Bill wasn't that good with babies. Too bad she wasn't closer. She'd be a perfect tester for Mommy Knows.

"Good for you, Becca. You're always so organized and smart."

Actually, I'd had to help her through algebra, and she'd only squeaked by with a D.

"Sorry I woke you. I'll let you go. I need to go get my baby, anyway. Bill couldn't change a diaper if his life depended on it. Oh! Speaking of which. You datin' anybody?" she asked.

"No. No, I'm not."

She didn't need to know about Brodie, and she certainly didn't need to know about Simon. That story would make her head explode. Green card marriages just didn't happen where I grew up.

"Good night then," she sing-songed.

After that disruption to my evening, I couldn't get back to sleep.

I tossed and turned, tormented by the thought that I might have gotten a life Becca never could have imagined. Granted, I'd made it happen with hard work, and a little selling of my soul—as in the marriage to Simon—but was it fair?

On the other hand, she could actually be perfectly happy with her life. Hell, maybe she felt sorry for *me*, living up here in the big, bad city with no husband or kids.

Everyone made their trade-offs.

CHAPTER 18

BRODIE

What an evening. A beautiful night with a gorgeous woman, delicious food and wine. And I'd fucked her senseless.

Or should I say she fucked me senseless? She was the one who'd taken control, after all.

Which was fine by me. In fact, thinking about it even now gave me a raging hard-on. There was nothing like a woman taking over, and knowing she wants you more than anything. Christ almighty.

I got to the hotel extra-early Saturday morning since I'd taken off early Friday. I didn't have any calls or texts, and no news was always good news, but I liked to keep an eye on things over the weekend.

And I had been feeling particularly protective of the hotel since I'd found out my partners were up to no good.

When I arrived, I went straight to Joel's office. Before I entered, I knocked. The last thing I wanted was to walk in on him fucking Pam. If they were still doing each other. Which they'd better not be.

"Come in!" Joel called. "Brodie, where were you last night? I can't remember the last time you missed a Friday here."

"I had other plans," I answered.

He broke out in a huge grin. "Dude. You dating somebody? Who is she? Tell me."

He leaned back in his chair, hands behind his head.

I took the seat opposite his desk. "Her name is Nara." He didn't need to know any more than that.

He held his hands out, palms up. "That's it? That's all you're giving me? Brodie, you're killing me." He looked at me expectantly.

"Okay. Okay, buddy, I get it. Let's go over the weekend." He flipped a few papers around on his desk and pulled something up on his computer.

"Do we have any VIPs coming in, Joel?"

"We do. Last night was quiet, celebrity-wise. But tonight, we have Aerosmith coming in. They have a show at the Garden."

Shit, I wish I'd known about that. I'd have gotten tickets. One of the perks of being a hotelier was easy access to backstage passes.

"Oh, one other thing. I almost forgot. The annual Spinsters party is on tonight."

"Oh damn, I nearly forgot about that one. I may go. What about you?" I asked.

He nodded slowly. "I might. Not sure yet. May have plans." He looked up at me guiltily.

"Oh for chrissakes. Are you still doing Pam? Wait, never mind. I don't want to know. I'm leaving right now."

"Okay, Brodie, thanks for stopping by—"

Who was I to say anything? I mean I'd messed around with chicks at work before, the most recent being Sonya. Joel could do what he wanted. I just didn't want to know about it and I didn't want him doing it in my penthouse suite.

I went to my office and texted Nara.

hey gorgeous. up for a party tonight?

I wasn't sure if she'd respond right away. Given that she was at work, she could be up to her elbows in baby shit.

that sounds great. when and where? and what to wear?

i'll pick you up at eight. dress sexy. like always.

:O

I was on my game. And that seriously felt good.

I drove my Telsa to Brooklyn to get Nara since the limo driver had the weekend off. When I pulled up to her place she walked out, wearing this long slinky number tied behind her neck, plunging into a deep V below her gorgeous breasts. She wore some sort of high-heeled sandals, and her hair was long and loose. I sprang a hard-on so big I almost couldn't get out of the car. I buttoned my sports jacket to cover the evidence and grabbed her hand as she descended the last steps of her building.

"Yowsa," I said, greeting her on the sidewalk with a long, slow kiss.

"You don't look too bad yourself, Mr. Hotel."

"Thanks, Miss Happy."

We walked to my car, and she stopped, hands on hips. "No way. Are you actually driving? Like driving a car? With four wheels?"

I rolled my eyes. "Believe it or not, yes. The driver's off for the weekend. Besides, I kind of miss being behind the wheel."

I helped her into the car, and we headed back toward the hotel.

She had her hand on my thigh as we worked our way over the Brooklyn Bridge and back to the city. Thanks to her, my hard-on raged the whole drive. That would need addressing later.

The Spinsters' party was held every year in our biggest ballroom, and let me tell you, I always looked forward to this shindig, which was full of New York's most beautiful women.

I'm not sure why they called themselves The Spinsters since they were anything but. The only thing they had in common with old maids was that they were mostly unmarried.

I said *mostly,* because the party was such a hot ticket that some women would lie about their marital status to get in. Couldn't say I blamed them. It was one of the city's biggest social events.

On top of providing serious eye candy, this group hired the best party planners in town, and this year's setup did not disappoint. When Nara and I walked in we were left speechless, so blown away we were by the décor.

It amazed me what people could do with a hotel ballroom, even when it was in my own hotel.

There were intimate seating areas set up all along the periphery of the room.

White sofas, loveseats, and benches were clustered around tables lit by flickering votive candles, that held buckets full of champagne, and platters of hors d'oeuvres.

It was like a dozen private little clubs.

And as if that weren't enough, special lighting made glittery reflections across the floor, up the walls, and over the ceiling. The effect was like being under water.

"Wow." Nara slowly took in the dramatic setting.

I put my arm around her waist and pulled her closer.

Nuzzling her ear, I said, "Wow is right. You are the most gorgeous thing in this whole party."

She dropped her head back and let out that laugh I loved, both elegant and down to Earth at the same time. And I was right.

She was the most beautiful woman there.

"Brodie!" a voice shrieked in my ear. Before I knew it, I'd been pulled free of Nara and caught in the bear hug of a female whose face I'd not yet seen.

"Hi," I said, trying to sound enthusiastic.

Nara just looked shocked.

"Darling, you never called me," the phantom hugger said, pulling away so I could finally see her face.

She was right. I hadn't called her. I had fucked her, but not called her. She had been nice enough and even pretty, but the night I'd met her, she hadn't stopped talking long enough for me to even learn her name.

That really bugged. Well, obviously it hadn't bugged

enough to keep me from doing her, but I wasn't going to hang out with her again.

Funny thing was, as much as I'd whored around and enjoyed it, my desire to continue doing so was suddenly tempered. What was that all about?

Nara extended her hand to the talker. "Hello," she said, smiling.

The woman's smile faltered as she looked Nara up and down. "Do we know each other?"

"No," Nara said with the world's sweetest smile and dropped her hand. "And I don't think we will."

She hooked her arm through mine and led me away.

That's my girl.

As we walked through the party, heads turned and nodded. I introduced Nara to those I thought she would enjoy meeting.

Even so, more than one woman looked her up and down and turned to their friends for a quick debrief. I wished Nara wasn't subject to this petty bitchiness and realized I probably wouldn't be back for next year's party.

In fact, I didn't think we'd even hang out at this one for very long.

"Brodie!" Joel said with Pam on his arm. Jesus, those two were indiscrete.

"Hey, Joel. Pam." I introduced them to Nara.

Pam placed a hand on Nara's arm. "Nara, let's run to the ladies' for a sec while the guys talk business."

"Um. Okay." Nara looked at me with raised eyebrows and turned to go with Pam.

Joel nudged me like the frat boy that he was.

"Yo, Brodie. You done good there. She's a looker. She another one of your trust fund babies?"

He had no idea how annoying he was. And he seemed to be forgetting that I was the boss.

"She's founder and CEO of a tech firm." I nodded to the mayor as he passed by with his usual entourage of beautiful women.

"No shit? I don't know any chicks who are tech anything, much less CEOs. Damn."

I hadn't known any, either. But I sure as hell was glad I did now.

CHAPTER 19

NARA

For some reason, I let a woman I'd just met, Pam, drag me off to the ladies' room.

I guess I was caught up with being polite. She had hooked her claws through my arm like we were best friends, and led me through the noisy, tipsy crowd.

One dude stepped right in front of me and shook his finger to start a drunken conversation. But good old Pam nipped that in the bud as she directed me into the restroom like I didn't know how to pee on my own.

I would rather not have left Brodie's side.

The Spinster party he'd brought me to was full of New York's best and beautiful—as well as the biggest bitches on wheels I'd ever seen. I'd never been scrutinized and looked up and down so much. Not that I minded a whole lot. I was pretty confident. But it was unsettling to have people looking at me like they wished I'd curl up and die.

That, I was not used to.

"So, Nara. Such an interesting name," Pam said, holding the bathroom door open for me.

But the look on her face said anything but interested.

"And you and Brodie make such a good-looking couple."

"Thank you. That's very nice of you to say." Not sure where she was going with all that, but I figured I'd have some fun with her.

"So look." She placed a patronizing hand on my arm. "I felt it was my responsibility to tell you not to get your hopes up about Brodie."

Probably best not to laugh in her face. With wide eyes, I said, "Thank you for letting me know that."

My feigned interest egged her on. She was practically gleeful.

"You see," she whispered conspiratorially, "he's just such a ladies' man, and is still not done sowing his oats."

I nodded and whispered back, "Good to know. Thanks for looking out for me."

She touched up her lipstick in the bathroom mirror, looking awfully pleased with herself. "Happy to help. I just felt you should know."

She fluffed her hair.

I could think of a few things *she* should know, but I wasn't going to waste my breath. Like what a great fuck he was, and how we'd shared some of our darkest secrets...

"Should we go back to the guys?" I asked.

She sighed deeply. "Sure. We'd better. They'll start to wonder if we met someone new."

She threw her head back and cackled.

I dumped Pam and made a beeline for Brodie, whose gorgeous head towered over the crowd. I wasn't surprised to see a couple women batting their eyes at him, and his weird employee, Joel, was trying to get in on the action.

But as soon as Brodie saw me, he extended his hand and caught mine in his large palm, bringing my fingers up to his lips in the most gallant freaking gesture I'd ever seen.

I'm sure the women watching assumed I was just his flavor of the week. And maybe I was. But I could have fun for a week.

I was a big girl.

He leaned toward my ear. "Hey, wanna take a walk?"

A sexy tingle zapped through me, and I could swear I wobbled for a moment.

"Please."

He grabbed me by the hand, leaving Joel and Pam open-mouthed as if we couldn't possibly have fun without them.

We dodged cocktail dresses, expensive suit jackets, and trays of champagne as we headed toward a nondescript door that looked like it could be opened only from the other side. As we got closer, Brodie whipped out a laminated badge and waved it, causing it to pop open just enough for us to slip through.

The benefits of ownership, I guess.

As unremarkable as the door was, the hallway on the other side was even more so. It was as if the hotel was a beautifully decorated stage, and the rest—the backstage— was ordinary and dull.

Brodie led me from the stark white hallway to a stairwell, which we climbed to another maze of halls. We finally entered what that looked like a storage room with a huge window spanning an entire wall. I drew closer and found it overlooking the ballroom hosting the Spinsters' party.

A thousand dressed-up New Yorkers flirted and drank beneath us in a sea of mostly black clothing, with the occasional red or green dress adding color.

"Look at all those people," I said.

Brodie's arm fell around my waist. "It is a great view, isn't it? We come up here to check and see how our events are going. It's a great perspective."

I fished through my purse. "Can I take a quick photo?"

"Sure. Go for it."

I showed Brodie my great shot, a freeze frame capturing the party below. It miraculously omitted the unpleasantness that hadn't been able to follow us to our secret place.

We turned to each other and his palms smoothed over my cheeks, leaving me rubbing into him like a cat in heat. He ran a finger down my arm to my hand, which he clasped. With his other, he caressed the nape of my neck—kneading and releasing. My eyes fell closed.

Surprising me, he gripped a fistful of my hair, his lips crushing mine. By contrast, he held my other hand as if we were kids on a first date.

This man blew my mind. First, he rode around in a limo, but he stopped to check on a homeless man. Then, he was heir to a hotel fortune, but his dad was in prison. And last, he was working hard to make his business partners whole, even though they were scheming behind his back to get rid of him.

And from what I could tell, he handled it all with grace.

I could learn from this guy.

With a small tug, he pulled the bow of my halter dress, sending it slithering to the floor a silky puddle around my feet. He pulled back from our kiss to see he'd left me wearing nothing but a lace, strapless bra and matching thong panty.

"Can those people see us up here?" I asked, inching away from the window.

"Nope," he responded. "It's mirrored on the other side."

Oh, this could be fun.

"Well, in that case," I murmured, backing against the window until my ass cheeks pressed on it.

He followed me, leaning his hands on the glass just behind my shoulders. His weight ground me, his hard cock announcing itself. The man's hunger shot straight to my core, leaving my nipples hard and my clit heavy and swollen.

He lost himself exploring me, sliding my thong down my legs, helping me step out of it. I started to kick off my heels.

"No. Keep them on. You know I like that," he whispered.

Who was I to argue? I felt so sexy and beautiful under his touch. He could have done anything he wanted.

He squatted so he was eye level with my shaved pussy, and leaned close enough to just run his tongue between the opening of my wet lips. The room spun.

With one hand pressing the window behind me and the other on his head, it was all I could do to remain upright.

"Turn around," he demanded.

I opened my eyes. Since I was in no condition to do anything fast, I rotated my body by leaning into the window. Bared and vulnerable, I looked down on the crowd below and found myself wishing they could see us.

Naughty girl.

"Stand here," Brodie directed.

I took a step back, and he bent me at the waist. He kicked my feet apart, leaving my pussy and ass fully exposed.

"What if someone comes in?" I was only somewhat concerned. This was too much fun to stop.

"Good for them if they do," he mumbled as he buried his face in my ass.

His tongue ran up and down my slit in an erotic tease. To intensify the sensation, I pushed back against him and he lapped me more deeply. I panted almost to the point of hyperventilation, steadying myself against the big window with the dirty knowledge I was getting off while watching the crowd below. If they only knew.

He slipped a finger into my hungry pussy, and I cried out, bucking against him for deeper penetration. He gave me two more fingers, and the fullness had me losing my mind as I writhed against the glass before the oblivious partiers below.

If that wasn't fucking hot, I didn't know what was.

My breath came in pants and my hands started to slip on the glass. I pressed against it harder for purchase and my breasts hung heavy, swinging from Brodie's pumping. A pressure built in my pussy and I clenched the fingers buried in me until I could take no more.

"C'mon baby. Come on my hand. I want to smell you. I want to taste you."

His words sent me over the edge.

"God, Brodie." I moaned.

He had an arm around my waist, holding me in place while he finger banged me, not stopping until a second wave of orgasm crashed into me.

My knees buckled and moved me to a sofa where he pushed my legs up over his shoulders and crammed his cock all the way in me in one stroke. In my stupor I had neither noticed him open his trousers, nor the condom he put on.

And now he was balanced over me balls deep, slamming my pussy, and shaking the sofa. His mouth was on mine, absorbing my screams as he spread wide.

Just when I thought I might pass out, a deep rumbling erupted from his throat. He growled my name, pushed as deeply as he could, and held himself there, his cock pulsating deep inside me.

All I could see were stars, and then everything went dark.

CHAPTER 20

BRODIE

Christ, I'd never fucked anyone into oblivion before. Nara was turned on as hell, getting worked over in front of a window with a thousand people on the other side of it, and when she finally detonated.

She crumpled into my arms, her skin hot and coated with a sweet layer of perspiration. I carried her to a sofa, donned a condom, and finished the job.

Afterward, she couldn't speak, but clung to me like a lifeline. I gathered her onto my lap and patted her clammy face until she came to a few seconds later. She was beyond cute, all curled up in my arms and whimpering, wearing nothing but those damn high heels. No one ever would have guessed she was founder of a tech firm that was about to rocket to success.

I guess that's part of what I loved about her.

Oh shit. Did I say love?

Like. I meant *like.*

"Wow," she murmured, looking around the room. "You really are something, hot stuff."

"You're not so bad yourself, Miss Happy."

I helped her step back into her dress and I tied it behind her neck just as it had been before I'd devoured her. She ran her fingers through her mass of hair and pulled out a compact from her purse, possibly to make sure she didn't have mascara running down her cheeks.

Even if she had, I would have wanted to remember her this way, forever.

"You're beautiful, doll," I told her.

She put the compact away and gave me a look that almost made *me* pass out. It was one of warm appreciation, and if I wasn't losing my mind, *kindness*. I didn't know that was a thing much less a turn on, but it blew me away.

"Okay," she said, smoothing the wrinkles in her dress and taking my hand. "I think I'm presentable enough. Where to now?"

I cleared my throat, my cock coming back to life like it was obsessed.

"Home. With me."

On the way out of the hotel lobby, I saw Joel and Pam in the distance, arguing and rolling eyes at each other.

I could tell by the way Nara averted her head that she'd seen them, too, and didn't want to get sucked into their drama. We kept our heads down and walked as quickly as her high heels would allow.

Outside in the beautiful evening, I handed my valet ticket to the bellman.

"Well, look who we have here," said a voice out of nowhere.

I wasn't sure where it had come from, but it was spoken in a very distinct British accent.

But Nara seemed to know, because her grip on my hand tightened so hard I thought she might break my fingers. She inched closer to me.

I smelled her fear, and instantly slid into protection mode.

A wiry, funny-looking guy sauntered up to us, getting uncomfortably close enough to ooze his bad breath. Given the fact that Nara had moved nearer to me, he had ended up in my personal space as well. Which was his first mistake.

"Can I help you?" I asked him, stepping forward until he had no choice but to step back.

He looked at me with a sneer and then back at Nara.

A light bulb went off. He was the English fucker extorting her for ten grand.

"Simon," she hissed, looking around, "what are you doing here? This is completely inappropriate."

He threw his head back and laughed. Just like all dickheads did.

"Oh, that's *rich*, darling." The he turned to me. "I know who you are. I read all about you in *Page Six*. Mr. Harcourt, did you know you are holding the hand of my *wife*? My legal wife?"

Nara stepped between us in an attempt to diffuse a

situation clearly headed for ugliness. But I held out an arm to keep Simon away from her.

"Look," I said calmly, "I know who *you* are now that you've opened your big fucking mouth. And you might want to think about backing off, or this may not end well for you."

Nara looked nervously from Simon to me and back. "Now, guys…"

But in spite of my warning, Simon ignored me and closed in on her again.

"Look you little bitch," he spat. "You owe me. And if you don't come through, you will be ruined. And I will enjoy every second of it—"

I could only guess where he was going with that, because he never finished. With a quick jab from my fist, he'd fallen to the ground screaming in pain, blood pouring out of his nose.

Yup. I'd slugged him.

And I wasn't done.

I grabbed him by the lapels and pulled him back to his feet. He sputtered and swore, his eyes tearing from the pain.

"Simon? Can you hear me?" I asked.

He continued stammering.

"Simon. I need to tell you something really important. Are you listening?"

He made an attempt at a weak nod.

"Listen carefully. I don't like repeating myself. If I were *you,* I would not threaten Nara again. Do you hear me?"

I let go of his lapel and as soon as I did, he stumbled and landed back on his ass. He was shouting what were probably obscenities, but his hysterical state mixed with his accent rendered his noise indecipherable. It was just as well. I needed to walk away before I got in trouble for assault. If I wasn't already.

During the fracas, my car had arrived. The valet stood with his mouth as wide open as the car door, waiting for the fight to end, or us to get in the car, or both.

"Thanks, dude," I said, tipping him. I closed Nara's door and we headed home.

Nara didn't say a thing until after I'd parked the car and we'd walked to my place.

"This is your building?" she asked, looking up at the old, industrial space.

I looked up at it, too. I had to admit, I really loved it. "Yeah. It used to be a sewing factory or something like that back in the day."

"I pass buildings like this all the time, and I always wonder what they were before they were turned into residences. This is so cool."

Like most New York homes, it took three keys and a combination to get in. The old building had been subdivided into four apartments, and the high ceilings lent themselves to the ever-popular open and airy loft configuration. I was a big fan of white walls and shiny black floors.

"Can I get you something to drink?" I asked.

"Sure. That would be great. What are you having?" She wandered around and checked my place out. She slid a couple books off my shelves, replaced them, and moved on to some family photos.

"Good question." I surveyed my liquor cabinet. What was I in the mood for...?

"I'm opting for a scotch. Care to join me?"

"Oooh, sounds good. I'd love one."

A woman who drinks scotch. What planet did she fall off of?

We settled into my oversized sofa.

"Well," she started, "that was something back there."

I nodded slowly, unsure about whether I was about to get a scolding or a pat on the back. I was ready for either.

She tilted her head. "Do you think he'll leave me alone now?"

"I don't know. He's an angry little shit. And borderline crazy, if you ask me. I doubt he'll just go away. If you continue to have trouble from him, let me know."

She smiled, and if I didn't know better, was teary eyed. "Thank you for defending me."

"It's always a pleasure to put a jerk like that in his place. And to help a kick-ass woman at the same time."

She set her drink on the coffee table and stood.

"Do you think I could see the bedroom?" she asked.

I was liking this woman more and more.

CHAPTER 21

NARA

After my sexy session with Brodie on the secret room overlooking the Spinsters party, I wanted more.

And then there was his apartment. Old-timey casement windows stretched the length of every exterior wall, their slim metal frames painted a lumpy black from years of coats of paint. The effect was utterly charming. An open kitchen sat in a far corner, and the rest of the first floor was so large there were two different seating areas and a dining room.

After a couple sips of my scotch, I was ready for the bedroom.

I was not usually the aggressor, but something about this man did me in. I wasn't in the market for a boyfriend or to even start dating for that matter, but just looking at him made my heart pound, and the way he looked back at me made me woozy.

It was as if he'd never seen a woman before, which of course, wasn't true—but without even trying, he made me feel…special.

Yes, that's what it was. Like I was really something. Who wouldn't love that?

Because his place was a loft, of course there was a set of stairs that led to another open space. Not only did I want more of him, I was dying to see the rest of the apartment—I'd never been in a loft. So I got bold, and led him by the hand.

The entire second floor was a wide-open bedroom overlooking the lower level. His unmade king-size bed was covered with what looked like the world's fluffiest down comforter, and a sofa and chair faced a wall-mounted TV in the corner. A grouping of framed photos on the wall drew me closer.

"Is that you?" I asked, pointing at a tall, lanky teenager who was handsome beyond his years while retaining the out-of-proportion puppy look so many adolescent boys wore.

"Yeah." He laughed. "I was pretty damn awkward."

"What? You?"

No way. Guys like him were never awkward. They were born to rule with their good looks and confidence.

"You probably had a gazillion girlfriends," I told him.

I, on the other hand, did not have a single suitor in high school. Lots of sex, but sex does not a relationship make. I learned that fact young and I learned it the hard way.

He shook his head. "I had crushes. Typical summer romances. I married my college girlfriend."

"You've been married? Really?"

"Yeah. We split after a year. We were too young. Too stupid."

Another surprise.

I moved toward him. Gripping his shirt, I untucked it from his trousers, my hands flying to his powerful chest.

In my heels, I still had to look up to see him. When I did, his mouth came down hard on mine, crushing my lips with a fury that both scared and thrilled me.

I slipped his jacket from his shoulders and worked the buttons of his starched shirt. He pulled me against his hips, his giant hard-on pressing against my abdomen.

It was as if it was our first time, and that we hadn't just fucked just an hour ago.

"You're beautiful, Happy. So fucking beautiful," he murmured in between kisses.

God, what this guy did to me. It should have been illegal.

I threw his shirt to the floor and my hands wandered to his strong back where I found his skin fevered. Almost too hot to touch.

Next, I went for his belt, my shaking hands bumping against the huge tent in his pants. He ran his own hands through my hair, grabbing fistfuls and burying his face in it.

He stood before me in his boxers, his perfect splay of chest hair winding down to that little line below his belly button, beyond which even greater treasures waited. I ran a finger along the waistband of his boxers, and his stomach muscles flexed as he gave a throaty growl.

I reached for the cheeks of his hard ass. I was

desperate to feel as much of him as I could so I closed my eyes, running my hands over every inch of flesh within my reach.

With a flick of his wrist, my dress puddled around my feet again.

He backed me up to the bed until I had to sit on its edge. Hooking his thumbs into the waistband of his boxers, he pushed them down his long, toned legs, his abs flexing as he bent and straightened.

His thick cock bounced in freedom, a drop of pre-cum hanging on its tip. Without meaning to, I moaned, again made dizzy by the pure masculine command in front of me.

"Taste me," he murmured, reaching to unhook my strapless bra.

When he did, my tender breasts hung free, craving his attention. But that would have to wait.

I held his cock in my two hands, amazed once more by its velvety length and prominent crown. I drew it into my mouth, getting it nice and wet, taking the entire length until it hit the back of my throat. I forced myself to relax to avoid gagging, and looked up to see his head loll back from the pleasure.

His hands wandered to my shoulders for leverage, his hips rocking to meet my demanding hunger.

He stiffened more, stretching the recesses of my mouth. My lips pistoned over the length of his shaft, resting occasionally on his swollen head. There, I increased my suction to a point that drove him to shout my name.

I was shaking with the power of our exchange and

sucked him harder, my cheeks hollowing from the force. Reaching a hand between my legs, I spread my slick cream over my hard clit, stroking it in time to my sucking.

His cock swelled and lengthened one last time.

"Suck me," he growled and shot fiercely into my mouth.

I swallowed as best I could, the rest of his thick cum running down my chin and landing on my breasts.

He fucked my mouth with one last thrust and leaned to kiss the top of my head.

I'd given other guys head before, but it had never made me so hot I had to be forced to stop.

"God, baby. Look what you did to me."

He tilted my chin up and I saw him dripping with perspiration, his hair soaked like he'd been out in the rain. He lifted me to standing with his strong arms and brought me to the bathroom where he wiped us both down with towels.

"C'mon. Under the covers," he said, leading me to bed.

Pulling the comforter up, he flicked off his bedroom light and wrapped his arms around me from behind. I sank into the safety of his embrace, where we remained until morning.

CHAPTER 22

BRODIE

That night I dreamt of my dad, and how all the bad stuff had gone down.

"Brodie, I need to talk to you."

I look up from the books I was working on, where I was learning how the hotel's accounting worked. My dad always wanted to make sure I knew every aspect of running the business.

"You have to know how to do this, son, so you can teach others," he had assured me as he had every year, starting back in the miserable summer when he had my fifteen-year-old self cleaning rooms.

That had been one lousy assignment, but boy, did I get a new appreciation for the housekeepers who hustled around the hotel, working their asses off.

"Yeah, Dad?" I asked, not looking up from the financial statement I was trying to put together.

"Son, you know how last year we had a shortfall of cash?"

I looked up from my work. "What about it?"

He looked down at his hands. He had an expression on his face that I couldn't read. Something was not right.

"Well, I took out a couple lines of credit."

"Okay. We've done that before, right?" I asked.

"Yes, we have. But this time, I didn't put the money where I should have—to pay the hotel's outstanding bills."

"What do you mean? What else would you do with the money?"

His eyes got red, and he looked up at the ceiling.

"Dad? What happened? What's going on?"

His voice cracked. "I...had to use it for some bills at home."

"What? Why?"

"Well, I got behind on a few things and thought I'd be able to pay it back before anyone noticed."

"You're gonna pay it back, Dad, right? I mean, can't you just pay it back?"

He shook his head and covered his face with his hand. "I can't. I can't."

My heart started to pound. The line of credit wasn't his to take. He had business partners he was accountable to...

"Okay. What do we do then?" I asked. I was sure there was a way to rectify the situation. We just needed to figure it out.

"It's too late, Brodie. I'm so sorry. I'm so sorry."

A sob escaped his mouth and tears ran down his face. The pain he was in hit me like a knife to my own chest.

He continued, "The business partners know. They're pressing charges. I may go to prison."

"Dad, how could you keep this from me? How could you... how could you..."

Somebody was shaking me, but when I looked around my dad was gone.

"Brodie. Sweetie, wake up. You're having a bad dream," Nara said, stroking my hair.

I looked around the dark room, still disoriented. "But my dad…my dad…"

"Shhh. Let's go back to sleep. It was a dream…"

Morning came too soon, the dream about my father still fresh as if Nara had woken me from it only five minutes earlier. She lay with her eyes wide open.

"How long have you been awake?" I asked her.

"Oh, not long. Just enjoying how sunny this place is."

She sat up in bed and the sheet fell to her waist, revealing her delicious breasts. I felt a twitch as my cock said good morning. I reached for her and pulled her back down.

"Hey, I gotta get up soon," she protested.

"I do, too. But we have a few minutes."

I propped myself onto my side and made circles around her pink nipple, which immediately sprang to attention. Like something else in the bed.

"You had a nightmare last night."

"I did. All that stuff from my dad came rushing back. Like your body stores it and springs it on you every now and then."

"What happened in the dream?" she asked.

"He was telling me what he'd done. I was so devastated

first, that he did it, and second, because it happened right under my nose."

I hadn't realized how worked up it still got me.

"You don't blame yourself, do you?"

I thought for a sec.

"For the longest time, I did. I guess I still do to an extent. That's why I want to repay my business partners, my dad's partners' sons. But Dad had done such a good job of hiding it; I don't know how long it would have taken me to find the discrepancies. The business partners only found out by accident when the bank had called one day when they couldn't get through to my dad. Guess it was a blessing that an end was put to it. But it was also the beginning of his being labeled a criminal."

She shook her head. "That must have been horrible."

"Still is. Causing nightmares and all. It's funny. I haven't had that dream in a long time."

"Glad I was here to wake you."

I pulled her close to feel those lush lips. They were comforting and a turn on all at once as evidenced by the way my hard cock.

We both had busy days ahead. But they could. The work would still be there.

I sent Nara home in an Uber since I liked to do a pass-through at the hotel on Sundays just to make sure the place was in decent shape after a busy Saturday night. As I settled into my office, my cell rang.

It was my attorney, Joe. Why was he calling me on a Sunday?

"Joe? What's up?"

"Did you have a run-in with a guy named Simon Robinson last night?"

That English shithead.

"I did. He threatened my date, Nara. I slugged him."

"Well, it seems he's pressing charges."

Oh, for chrissakes.

"That little fucker. You know what he's doing to her—"

"Brodie, I don't care what he's doing to anyone. My job is to keep *you* out of trouble. Please don't go hitting people."

Goddamn. Why hadn't I killed that little weasel? Well, because then I'd be headed to prison.

Just like my father.

"Brodie? Can I get your word? That you won't go hitting anyone else?"

"Yes, Joe, of course. You're right. I had a lapse in judgment."

"Cool. Okay, I'm getting back to my Sunday. Tomorrow I'll work on getting the charges dropped. Be a good boy."

"Will do, Joe. Thanks for calling."

Perhaps I'd had a lapse in judgment in trying to take care of Simon on my own.

Next time, maybe I'd have someone else handle him for me.

～

"Dalt."

It was early to be calling my brother in San Francisco, but I needed to talk.

"Bro, what's up?" he asked with a big yawn.

"Hey man, sorry I woke you," I said.

"You okay? All good out there on the East Coast?" he asked me.

"Yeah. I suppose." I leaned back in my chair and closed my eyes.

"I'm glad you called," he said. "I think I've got some investors for you to talk to."

I sat up straight in my chair. "Get the hell out. You're kidding me."

"No, man. They're heavy hitters and they trust my judgment. I think they'd like to invest in a property in San Francisco and New York."

My heart was pounding so hard it made my head hurt.

"Dude. Are you shitting me?" I asked.

"Put together a proposal, show off what you've done with Hotel Vertigo, and I think you'll be able to sell them."

"Holy shit, Dalt. You are fucking kidding me."

My head reeled with the possibilities.

Maybe everything would be okay. Could I even hope?

It had been so long.

CHAPTER 23

NARA

"Mom, I have to be honest with you. I'm not coming back for the reunion. I don't care that Becca told everyone I'd be there."

How many more times did I have to say that?

She sighed loudly. "Everyone is counting on seeing you. I don't see how you can let your friends down."

Shoot me know.

"I saw Becca the other day. Her children are beautiful, and she seems so happy."

"Good. I'm glad she's happy. She doesn't need me to come to town. No one does. They'll have the reunion and no one will ever miss me."

My mother was silent for a moment. "I'll miss you."

There it was.

"Oh, Mom, I miss you, too. Just let me know when you want come to New York. We'll have a great time. And please stop telling Becca I'm going to come. Because I'm not."

"If that's what you want, sweetie. But I think you'll be missing out on a lot of fun."

We obviously had different ideas about fun.

I figured I had some version of "survivor's guilt."

Obviously no one had died, but the guilt of having escaped my hometown, having left it behind like I did, made me feel like a scumbag.

But I'd had no choice—I would have slowly died there. My only ties to the place, Becca and my mom, were growing weaker every year.

The longer I lived in New York, and the more life rolled onward, the more unlikely it was I'd ever go back. There was no going home, as the old saying went. I didn't know who the hell would want to, anyway.

I'd not heard from Simon since the night Brodie had punched him out. I honestly wished it had never happened, but I had to admit—it did feel good to have someone defend me.

Problems like Simon were a lot easier to contend with when someone had your back.

Especially someone like Brodie.

But I had a nagging feeling Simon wasn't permanently out of my life yet. Hard as I tried to shake it off, it followed me around like a dark cloud.

Joi poked her head into my cubicle.

"Hey," I said.

She bounded in, blond hair flying, scooping up a pile of papers to make room for herself.

"So, how are you feeling about things? I mean, are we ready for our meeting?"

"I think so. At least as ready as we'll ever be."

My head was pounding, but everything else was great.

We had investors from a venture capital firm coming by in an hour along with several beta testing moms who'd be joining to help demonstrate the Mommy Knows software app. Well, their babies would be helping, too.

Mimi had lined up ten moms; out of the group, someone's baby would certainly pee or poo. In a show of support, some even offered to give their little ones an additional bottle just prior to the meeting to help facilitate the messy diapers we so desperately needed.

It was a real team effort.

This was an all-hands-on-deck type of day. Even the introverted software engineers tidied up their work areas, wore something other than ratty hoodies, and were ready to be friendly.

There'd been plenty of grousing, but when I reminded the complainers about their stock options and the potential for making money, they shut right up.

Mimi had arranged for catering, so we had snacks and beverages to offer. I didn't want to go too crazy, since we'd be talking about dirty diapers after all.

We'd researched the team coming in, and several of them were parents—what luck. They'd get the gist of what we were doing in a second. Moms and dads always did.

"Anyway, what about the new guy, Mr. Hotel?" Joi asked with a raised eyebrow.

"He's great," I said simply.

She rolled her eyes. "C'mon. Don't be stingy. Share."

The thought of Brodie made my heart race—not a comfortable state for me.

"We've had some really nice times together…"

"Oh, I can hear it," she said. "Here it comes…dum da dum dum…what's wrong with him? What did he do?"

"He's fine, he's done nothing wrong. I'm just not sure about getting involved. I can't afford any time away from the business right now."

There was more behind my hesitation, but I hadn't put my finger on it yet.

Confusion marked Joi's pretty face. No, she didn't know how relationships took time. She'd always had Jack, so she had nothing to compare it to.

"Well, there was also an incident," I added.

She scooted forward on her chair, eyes widened.

"I knew it! Tell me everything."

"He punched out Simon."

"Oh. My. God." She looked as though she'd just won the gossip lottery.

I told her the whole story while she shook with excitement.

"That is so badass. Nara, you gotta give this guy a chance. He sounds awesome."

"Yeah, thanks. I think I'll be able to figure it out."

Hurt crossed her face. I needn't be such a bitch to her.

But I hated being pushed.

Two hours later, I was fairly floating.

Not only had several of the babies done both number one *and* number two, the sensor strip in their diapers had communicated perfectly with the moms' smartphones.

Things could not have gone better, and if these investors weren't all over the promise of Mommy Knows, well they could go to hell. They'd be missing the opportunity of a lifetime.

My phone buzzed.

how was the big meeting, beautiful?

He'd remembered!

beyond perfect. seriously

i knew you'd knock it out of the park

thank you

Oh my god, I was melting. He did that to me, dammit.

My resolve to remain single and unfettered was weakening by the day. I hadn't been this terrified of anything in a long, long time.

you should be getting your divorce papers soon from simon. then you'll never hear from him again.

what do u mean?

I had some friends take care of the matter.

Oh my god oh my god oh my god.

brodie what did u do?

don't worry about it. ur all set now.

What the hell? Did he kill the guy? Or just turn him into a vegetable?

can you call me?

My phone rang right away.

"Brodie, what do you mean, I won't hear from Simon anymore?"

My heartbeat pulsed in my temple for the second time that day, only this time, it was worse. And on top of it, I felt like vomiting.

"Baby, I told you I took care of it." He sounded as casual as if he'd just ordered take-out.

"Tell me what is going on. Did you do something to Simon?"

He laughed. "I guess you could say that."

But I wasn't laughing. "I don't like the sound of this. Tell me what happened."

My voice shook, and I swallowed hard to hide it.

"I sent someone to have a talk with him. That's all. But it was a firm talk. It was made very clear he wasn't to bother you ever again. And if he did, the consequences would be very, very serious."

No fucking way.

I exploded. "What are you, in the mafia or something? You break people's legs?"

I was so pissed I gripped the edge of the desk until my knuckles whitened.

"Hey, what's the big deal? I had a problem taken care of. Apparently the asshole was scared shitless. It's over."

"I don't appreciate that." I said.

There was silence for a moment.

"What? What do you mean?" he asked, incredulous.

Amazing how clueless guys could be.

"It was not up to you to resolve my problem with

Simon. You may have just made a bad situation much worse."

I needed to lower my voice.

"You're joking right?" Now his voice was tense. "You're *not* happy that asshole is off your back?"

"I am not happy you interfered with my situation. I appreciate your wanting to help but threatening him was completely inappropriate."

"Wow. Okay," he said.

I could picture him running his hand through his hair, baffled beyond understanding.

"Okay," he began slowly. "I…guess I fucked up. I…I am sorry. I overstepped."

Brodie had overstepped because I'd let him overstep. He thought I was a damsel in distress. That I needed saving.

Well, he was wrong.

And I'd been wrong to let down my guard.

CHAPTER 24

BRODIE

Well, I'll be damned.

It had never occurred to me that Nara might not want me to rough up the little English punk who'd been making her life miserable.

My hotel security had tracked him down. While I wasn't there to witness the conversation, they'd apparently put the fear of god in him as per my instructions.

If there was one thing I couldn't stand it was betrayal. I was all too familiar with it, having experienced it in the depths of my soul. I didn't want to see Nara suffer it the way I had.

But Christ if she wasn't pissed that I'd tried to help. I had not anticipated that. Maybe I was so caught up being a knight in shining armor that I'd lost my perspective. And maybe I was so unused to dating smart, confident women, I hadn't realized one of them might not need the kind of help I could offer.

Now I was kicking myself.

Why hadn't I thought things through more carefully?

Protecting someone I liked was instinctual. So was making a messed up situation right.

That's why I was working so hard to ensure the guys swindled by my father were made whole. And sometimes it seemed that as hard as I tried, I wasn't making anyone happy in the end.

Now I was in the doghouse with Nara, and it looked like I might be there a long time, if not forever.

There was a knock at my office door, and Trudy stuck her head in. "I'm getting ready to head out for the night. Do you need anything else?"

"No, Trudy. Thank you."

I needed something, but not anything Trudy could give me.

~

The hotel lobby was in its usual pristine state.

The marble shone like glass, the huge flower arrangements were balanced to perfection, and the staff floated across the floor, making sure every guest need was attended to. It was no accident this was the best hotel in town.

I watched the front desk from across the floor where Sonya was checking in some young actor whose name I couldn't recall.

Always the professional, she didn't bat an eye at celebrities, showing no more reaction for a famous rock star than she would for a mom from New Jersey in for a girls' weekend.

I appreciated that about her.

"Sonya, how are you today?" I asked when she was free.

She licked her full lips, and I felt a twitch in my trousers.

"Oh, Mr. Harcourt. Hello." She looked down at her hands as her face turned a bright pink.

Her coworker, Scott, summoned the next guest over so she could speak with me.

"Sonya, I told you to call me Brodie."

"You're right. I'm sorry. It's just that in our staff meetings they refer to you as Mr. Harcourt. So that's just what I automatically call you."

"I see. Hey, is your shift ending right about now?" I asked.

She looked at her watch and her eyebrows rose in a knowing look. "Wow. I guess it ended about five minutes ago."

Finished with his guest, Scott said, "I've got it under control, Sonya, if you're wanting to take off." Awesome guy.

She looked at me and smiled, straightening up her workspace. Without a word, she exited through the door behind reception using her security key card. She held it open for me and I followed her in.

She was just so hot in her uniform, which stretched across her huge tits and accentuated her small, trim waist. She reached up, hooked her hands behind my head, and began kissing my neck.

But instead of devouring her as I would have in the past, my arms hung at my side, frozen.

All I could think about was Nara.

Shit. I removed Sonya's arms from my neck.

"I'm so sorry," I told her. And I left.

That night on my way home in the limo, I called my brother.

"Dalt," I said when he answered.

"Bro. Good to hear your voice."

"Hey, I'm ready to take some action on the hotel business."

"Yeah? What did you have in mind?" he asked.

"Couple things. One, I want to connect with your investors who are interested in San Francisco. And two, I think I'm gonna have my lawyer write up papers to buy out my partners' shares in Vertigo."

He exhaled hard. "Wow. Do you have the cash?"

"I'm not sure. That's why I was hesitating. I'll have to liquidate some investments. But it'll be fine. I'll get those douches off my back and out of my life."

Dalt breathed a laugh. "You probably should have done that from the get-go."

"Yeah, you're right. But partnering with them seemed like the right thing to do at the time. I know better now, since I discovered their plans to fuck me over."

"Sounds like you know what you've got to do, Bro."

Once home, I found the apartment painfully empty without Nara, and yet, her essence was as strong as if she'd never left.

Her faint perfume filled the air, a few of her long hairs lie on her pillow, and the glass by the side of the bed bore a hint of her lipstick.

God, I was turning into a pussy.

I wasn't sure whether I'd blown it with her, but my pride was chafed that my efforts had gotten me into hot water. I'd honestly thought I was doing the right thing in threatening Simon, and the caveman part of me was pissed she didn't appreciate it.

But the modern me realized that a woman as smart and accomplished as Nara didn't need my rescuing.

Hell, she'd developed her own software app and founded her own company. Sure, she'd married herself into a corner with a soulless prick, but she'd find her way out.

Just like I'd find my way out from under my business partners, and the HWE partnership.

CHAPTER 25

NARA

I was beside myself that Brodie interfered with my problems and threatened Simon.

For one, I didn't think any amount of threats would scare that little weasel off—that's how strong-willed he was. And second, where the hell did Brodie get off anyway?

How could he possibly have thought I'd be okay with one of his henchmen tracking Simon down and putting the fear of god into him? Life just didn't work that way. At least, not for me.

Pissing off Simon was like whacking a hornet's nest with a baseball bat. You might be trying to kill the damn thing, but you only ended up making matters worse.

That about summed up the man who was my husband. Faux husband. I couldn't risk having him ruin me. I needed to find a way to raise the ten grand. Ten grand I simply didn't have.

So there was that. But I was actually more furious with myself than with Brodie.

I'd vowed not to get involved, and then I had fallen into his rich, sexy clutches. I mean, no one had ever flown me in a freaking helicopter to the freaking Hamptons, for freaking dinner.

My vain ass had gotten sucked in by flattery and treats. I knew better than that.

Mommy Knows needed me. And I needed it. I didn't want some guy to throw a wrench into my hard-fought plans for world domination in the area of dirty baby diapers.

I knew what I had to do.

Simon's number rang and rang. So I left a voicemail message.

"Hey, Simon, it's Nara. Listen, Brodie told me he sent someone to talk to you, and I just wanted you to know I didn't know about it until just now. I'm sorry he harassed you. Will you call me to talk?"

I didn't know what would come of my effort to reach Simon.

I suspected it wouldn't be anything good, but I had to at least try to keep things from getting worse.

Joi popped into my cube and made herself at home like she always did.

"What's up, bitch?" she said, laughing.

"Hey, don't say that so loudly here. It's not a good example for the rest of the team. We're in management, remember?"

She rolled her eyes.

"Management shmanagement. They're cool," she said, waving her hand around in her *no big deal* manner.

But it *was* a big deal. I was trying to build a damn company. She was my best friend, but sometimes I wondered if she understood what a great opportunity we were on the brink of.

I changed the subject to something that would not include her calling me *bitch*.

"So how's the wedding planning?" I smiled to show how interested I was. Not.

She brightened. Because, of course.

"Ohmygod, I'm super excited. Just two more weeks. And"— she paused as if waiting for a drumroll—"I've lost five more pounds."

She was looking a little drawn. "Just don't lose any more weight. Your boobs will become concave."

Her hands flew to her chest. "Eh. I never had much in that department. We're not all as lucky as you," she said, pointing at my chest.

"Speaking of lucky," she continued, "what's up with your hotel guy? He sweep you off your feet, yet?"

I told her about his tracking down Simon to "put the fear of god in him." Whatever that meant.

Her eyes nearly popped out of her head. "No way! He doubled down!"

"I guess he did," I said flatly.

"That is super hot."

It took her a moment to realize I felt differently. "Wait. You're not happy about him stepping in?"

"Not everyone wants to date a caveman," I explained.

She shrugged. "Suit yourself. He sounded like a nice guy. I'm sure his intentions were good." She stood to leave.

I wondered what work she wasn't getting done by hanging out with me. But then, I wasn't getting any work done, either.

I shook my head. "He *was* a nice guy. But it's over now."

"Ugh. You're an idiot sometimes."

What?

I chafed at her name-calling. But maybe she had a point.

"Well, he pissed me off. Like I couldn't handle my own shit." I looked up at her. "I founded my own company, for heaven's sake."

"Yeah, but you also broke the law with a fraudulent marriage. You're not perfect, just like he is not," she said.

Fraudulent marriage. Those very words made the acid in my stomach churn.

Mercilessly.

Shoulda-woulda-coulda.

"How I wish I could do that whole bit over." I buried my face in my hands.

"Well, you can't. Time to face the music. Call Simon's bluff. I don't think he'll expose you, because he'd be deported. And if he did try to ruin you, I don't think he could. You have a stellar reputation and a strong product.

You might get fined by the INS, and that would suck, but I think your business partners would stand behind you. I know everyone here at the company would."

Tears stung at my eyes. Shit, I didn't want to cry over this. But it had added so much stress to my already over-loaded life. I was just done with it.

Joi saw my misery and sat back down.

"You can do this," she said.

Now, the tears were pouring down my cheeks. Might as well get them out. I no longer gave a shit if anyone else in the office could hear.

I was overdue for a pity party.

"I got out of that godforsaken little town I grew up in, but I keep getting pressured to go back. I sold my soul for ten grand, and now, I'm on the brink of being punished for that. My software app is still buggy, and can confuse the difference between pee and poo."

Joi and I looked at each other.

She was clearly trying to suppress a smile, and in doing so, her shoulders were shaking.

Then, my own smile grew, and as hard as I tried not to laugh, a snort escaped my nose.

Joi broke out into ear-splitting guffaws, and I followed. The harder we laughed, the harder it was to stop, until we were left gasping for air.

Mimi poked her head around the corner. "All good here?"

Unable to answer, I just nodded. She looked from me to Joi, rolled her eyes, and left.

Joi was right.

Brodie was only trying to help me. I don't know yet if

he'd done more harm than good, but his intentions were clear.

And he liked me.

Not thirty minutes later, Simon returned my call. But for the first time, I was ready to face him.

"Simon!" I couldn't have been more cheery.

"Well, if it isn't my darling wife," he growled.

Oops, looked like the hornet's nest was indeed irritated.

"Simon, I'm sorry about Brodie. He's such a hothead. I couldn't believe he slugged you like that."

Actually, I could totally believe it. What I couldn't believe was that I'd never done it myself.

In my most wide-eyed, innocent voice—if I even had such a thing—I said, "You weren't hurt, were you? I really hope you're okay."

The sweetness was sickening. And one hundred percent phony.

"I got my nosed plowed in, and you're asking if I'm fine?"

"It's terrible he did that," I purred sympathetically. "I couldn't believe my eyes."

"Bollocks, Nara. And I'm sure you know what happened after that."

His fury pounded in my ear.

"He did tell me he sent someone to speak with you. I don't know much more than that. But I didn't put him up to it, and in fact, I am pissed at him for interfering."

"Yeah, right. But it doesn't matter. I'm going to *Page Six* to tell them that you, their auction date darling, is actually a felon. All of New York will be interested in *that* story."

I swallowed hard, and then did the hardest thing I'd ever done.

"Go ahead, Simon. Feel free. I'm not paying you. Ever."

Silence.

"Okay, Nara. Have it your way. You'll be sorry, you will!"

"If you don't sign the divorce papers Simon, I'll be calling the INS, and you *will* be deported," I added calmly.

I pictured him sputtering and spewing, having a temper tantrum, and then being swallowed up by the Earth like Rumpelstiltskin. If only.

His voice escalated to a scream, forcing me to hold the phone away from my ear. "You little bitch. I'll ruin you!"

"No, Simon, you won't. *I* will ruin you. I may be fined, but I will remain in the United States. *You*, however, will not. So let me know what you decide. You know how to reach me."

As I went to hang up, the phone exploded in a string of obscenities so long and loud I couldn't make out a single one of them. But that didn't matter.

Not anymore.

Brodie had overstepped his bounds. But he'd succeeded in pushing mine.

I never would have told Simon off without him.

CHAPTER 26

BRODIE

For the first time in a long time, I had some clarity.

I called my broker to liquidate a big part of my investment portfolio, so I'd have the cash to buy out my partners. It was hard to do, but it wouldn't break me. Then I called my lawyer to put things in motion.

"Joe. Thanks for taking my call," I said.

"Always happy to hear from my favorite client. Hey, the guy you hit dropped the charges against you."

"Great. That's a relief. Thank you."

"You're welcome. It wasn't hard to get him to do. Funny how fast he changed his mind," Joe said.

It wasn't funny to me, but my attorney didn't need to know that.

"So what else is happening?" he asked.

"I've decided what I want to do about the partnership. I'm going to buy *them* out."

Hotel Vertigo was part of my family, and part of me. No one was taking it away.

I heard a low whistle. "Now you're talking. Let's take them on."

Relief washed over me. I hadn't been sure Joe would support my approach.

"All right. Can you start with filing the paperwork? I'm getting the cash together right now," I said.

"Sure thing, buddy. I'll round up the team and we'll get right on it."

"Thank you. I can always count on you."

When everything had gone down with my dad, Joe was one of the people who stuck by my family. You keep people like that around.

"Brodie, how long have I known you?"

"Long time, Joe."

"How about since you were a little kid? I'd do anything for your dad, or for you. You know that."

I choked down a lump in my throat.

"Thank you," I said simply.

"Now you know what you need to do. Get the actuary going on valuing the business. Everything else will fall into place."

I hoped he was right.

Next stop of the day was to make another situation right. I had the limo take me uptown to Nara's office.

I walked into a typical tech firm, with walls painted a

mish-mash of bright colors, cubicles for miles, and cheap Ikea furniture. It was textbook perfect.

A cheery receptionist greeted me.

"Hello! What can I help you with?"

"I'm Brodie Harcourt to see Nara Kincaid."

Her smile was blinding. "Does she have a meeting scheduled with you, Mr. Harcourt?"

"No. No she doesn't. I'm a friend. I hope she can see me for a few minutes."

That changed her demeanor, and she looked me up and down.

"I see. Hold on one sec." She disappeared through a door. I could hear her on the other side of it. Her voice was muffled, but enthusiastic, nonetheless.

The door flew open. It was Nara, wearing her usual uniform, but with her hair piled on her head, held in place with a pencil. How did she do that?

"Brodie," she said hesitantly. She broke into a smile and drew me into a hug.

Maybe I wasn't in as much trouble as I'd thought.

"Could we go somewhere to talk?" I asked.

"Yeah. Let's do that. I'll grab my purse, and we can get a drink at Bella Stella."

Ten minutes later, we settled into the bar where we'd met for the first time.

I ordered us a couple drinks—bubbly for her, and scotch for me. But I didn't wait for them to be served.

"I wanted to talk to you," I started.

Her eyes widened. "Funny. I wanted to talk to you, too. And then you showed up at my office."

We looked at each other for a moment, not sure where to go next.

So I dove in. "I'm sorry I got involved with your Simon problems. I never should have done that. You're perfectly capable of taking care of yourself."

Her mouth opened and closed a couple times before she could say anything.

"Oh gosh, Brodie," she sputtered. "Thank you for saying that. I'm sorry I came down on you so hard. You did something I didn't want you to, but you were only trying to help. Instead of losing my shit, I should have thanked you for caring. And then lost my shit."

She laughed.

Now it was my turn to be stunned. "Thank you. Wow. I...I didn't expect *that*."

"So," she said with a smile. "Let's move on from this. Okay?"

Shit, yeah.

"Speaking of moving on, are you free tonight?" I asked.

"No, but I'd love to get together," she said, smiling.

"Okay. That was confusing. But I'll take it as a yes."

"Yes," she said. "It was a yes."

I picked her up at eight. She walked out of her office building looking slamming as always with those never-ending long legs on skyscraper heels, and her uniform, which she wore painfully well.

She slipped into the limo next to me and laid a big kiss

on my lips. As usual, my dick twitched to remind me it was there.

Down, boy.

"Hello, beautiful," I said.

Even in the low light I was able to see her blush.

"Hey there," she answered with a smile.

"What do you feel like doing?" I asked.

She rubbed her chin for a moment. "I know! Let's do something naughty. I'm in the mood for naughty."

She looked to me like I was the expert in naughty, so I closed the window between the driver and us. "What put you in that mood?"

"Well," she said. "We just got over a major hurdle with the Mommy Knows software. I'm feeling very confident and gutsy."

"No kidding. What was the hurdle?"

"It was that one I told you about, where the dirty diaper sensor was reading wrong. It was mixing up its signals. And that's all you really want to know," she said, laughing.

"Okay. I think you're right. Dirty diapers are not really conducive to a naughty night out."

"I don't suppose they are. Actually, unless you absolutely have to, I'd recommend not talking about them at all, ever. Unless you're dealing directly with one and have no choice," she said.

Nothing like a smart girl with a sense of humor.

"Okay then," I said. "How naughty do you want to go?"

My dick was getting harder by the second.

"Gosh, I don't know. Are there a lot of options?"

Oh, my sweet, sweet girl.

"You're in freaking New York City, baby. The options are endless," I explained.

"Really? Well I guess I've been living under a rock."

"All right. First option. We could go to a strip club. A nice one, not a divey one," I offered.

"Oh, that's an idea. I've been to a strip club once before. On a dare," she added.

"Or...we could go to a sex club," I ventured, not sure how that would go over.

"A sex club? Like where people sit around having sex?" she asked.

"Something like that. Some people watch, some perform. It's whatever you feel like. And always consensual."

She looked out the window at the red light where we were stopped. At this point I didn't care if she was into it or not, just as long as I could get her naked, and soon.

Then she turned back to me. "Is it safe? I mean, will you stick with me?" she asked.

I threw my head back and laughed. I couldn't help it.

"Will I stick with you? Hell, yeah. Just try to get rid of me."

She reached across the seat and took my hand. "We could do that. I mean, I'd like to try it."

"If you don't like it, we'll leave right away," I offered.

"Let's go."

Cripes. I'd sought out Nara to offer a mea culpa, and even

do a bit of groveling if necessary to get back in her good graces.

And now we were heading across town to go to a freaking sex club.

There were several such clubs in Manhattan just like there were in every major city, and I'd been to a few of them with various kinky girlfriends. But never with someone as beautiful and elegant as Nara.

And never with someone who I was as determined to keep all to myself.

I had the limo stop at the end of a block, and we walked back a few addresses until we landed in front of a plain black door that blended in with the rest of the block. A large bouncer stepped out of the shadows, looked us up and down, and let us in.

We entered a long, dimly lit hallway.

At the end, a costumed woman waited in what looked like the ticket booth of an old movie theater. As we got closer, she smiled and slipped a few condoms onto the counter.

Nara looked surprised but slid them into her skirt pocket. I paid the admission, and we were buzzed in.

I could barely walk with the huge erection I'd already sprung—there was nothing sexier than the thought of fucking Nara in front of an audience.

CHAPTER 27

NARA

Holy shit, I was in a sex club.

I'd heard of places like this and had friends who'd been to them, but I'd never had the guts to go myself. Well, I'd never had anyone to bring me to one, either. But something about Brodie felt so safe, and it didn't hurt that he was sexy as hell.

If I hated it, we'd just leave. Easy.

After passing through two massive security doors, we entered a swanky lounge area with a dozen people perched on sofas and chairs, chatting and drinking cocktails.

I leaned close to Brodie's ear. "What's going on?"

"Most people warm up a little. They want to talk to other folks, see if there is anyone they want to play with."

I held his hand tightly. It *was* my first time after all.

"Some people stick with the partners they came with,

and some get into swapping." He pulled me close. It felt seriously good.

"But I plan to keep you all to myself," he whispered.

Hell, yeah.

We went to get a drink from a curvy bartender wearing a pink merry widow attached to garters and stockings, and theatrical makeup along the lines of Cirque du Soleil. The perfect look for a sex club.

She tilted her beret-covered head and looked us up and down with what I was pretty sure was approval.

"Two champagnes," Brodie told her as he handed her a couple twenties.

"Coming right up," she said with a big smile.

Seconds later, we had ice-cold bubbly in our hands. I was nervous and took a huge gulp. I was pretty sure Brodie sensed my nerves, because he led me to a sofa in a quiet corner.

"Let's just watch for a bit," he said.

I couldn't believe I was there. I wanted to play it cool, but really felt like jumping out of my skin.

I had to say, the other guests were for the most part very good looking—fit, well dressed, and classy. Would I see anyone I knew? God, I hoped not.

We watched for a while. Two hunky fireman-like men took a woman up some stairs. She looked pretty damn happy. Couldn't say I blamed her.

"Where are they going?" I asked Brodie, tipping my head toward the threesome.

"Probably to one of the playrooms upstairs." He turned to look at me. "You like that? Two guys?"

I looked around the room, and when my gaze returned to Brodie's, it was clear he was waiting for an answer.

"Um, yeah. I suppose."

I'd certainly thought about it before but had never pursued it. I mean, what do you do, put an ad on *Craigslist* and say you wanted a threesome?

Actually, that probably *was* what people did.

"Will you be okay here if I run to the restroom?" he asked me.

Ummmm…

I smiled brightly. "Of course. Just don't forget about me." I laughed bravely.

He bent to kiss my temple. "Be back in a flash."

I went to take another sip of my champagne and found the glass nearly empty.

Slow down, girl.

I leaned back on the sofa to take it all in, and a woman plopped down beside me. She was beautiful in a Cleopatra-sort of way, with black bobbed hair, blunt bangs, and heavy eye makeup.

I wondered if I could pull off a look like that.

"Hi," she said, hand extended. "I'm Aimee."

There was the slightest slur to her words.

I took her hand. "Nice to meet you."

She leaned too close. "You're awfully pretty."

I thanked her.

"Would you like to go upstairs and play around?"

Not only had I never been to a sex club, but I'd also never messed around with a woman. This might have been a night of firsts, but one thing at a time please.

I inched away from her on the sofa—somehow, she'd gotten even closer in the minute since she'd sat.

"Uh, well—" I sputtered.

"Excuse me, miss. Mind if I sit by my friend, there?"

Brodie!

Aimee's eyes widened at the sight of him. "Sure thing. I was just keeping her company." She stood on unsteady feet.

"Talk to you later," I said to her.

Brodie turned to me, his handsome face amused. "Look at you. I leave you for five minutes, and you have someone picking you up already."

The desire in his eyes was equaled by the massive hard on tenting his trousers.

"Well, seeing as this is a sex club, I suspect it's not that unusual."

The throbbing between my legs suggested the decision to join him had been a good one.

"Did you like her?" he asked.

I nodded. "Yeah. I did. She was hot. A little drunk, I think. But hot. Do you think I could pull off a look like that?"

"Shit, you could pull off any look you like. And do it a thousand times better."

I rolled my eyes. "Okay, Mr. Hotel. Flattery will get you everywhere."

He stood, extending his hand. His fingers dwarfed mine and were oh-so-warm.

I followed him upstairs to where I imagined all the magic happened.

~

The playroom was even more sexy than the lounge area.

Filmy curtains hung floor to ceiling, fluttering with the movement of people in the room. Large sofas and round mattresses were scattered about, covered in soft, plushy fabric.

What I really wanted to see was the woman who'd gone up the stairs with the two men.

"You good? You okay with this?" Brodie asked, squeezing my hand.

"Yeah," I breathed. "It's very cool."

I was staring. I couldn't help it.

We made a lap around the floor.

In one corner, a woman sat on a big cushy chair with her dress pushed up to her hips. A man knelt before her, his face buried between her legs.

He must have been pretty good at what he was doing, because the look on her face was one of pure ecstasy. She reached for his head and pulled him deeper, tossing her own head back and forth, bucking her hips, and releasing a moan that made me weak in my knees.

It was as if by watching her, I was experiencing her orgasm, too.

While I stood there, watching, Brodie pressed his lips to my neck. My skin exploded in goosebumps from his surprise attack. I turned to him, planting my hands on the sides of his gorgeous face, which was prickly from not having shaved since morning.

I couldn't wait to feel his rough skin burning the inside of my thighs.

It was so naughty. And thrilling.

Just then, one of the billowy curtains floated aside, catching my eye. There, behind it, were the two men and woman I'd seen downstairs.

Whoa.

The woman lay on her back with one of the men positioned by her head, his cock thrust in her mouth. The other man had one of her thighs draped over his shoulder, his hand invisible beneath her skirt. From the noises she made, I think it was safe to say his fingers were inside her, giving her the pleasure of her life.

"Hot, isn't it?" Brodie murmured in my ear.

"Um...yes," I swallowed, feeling dry. "Could we get another drink?"

"Sure, baby."

His arm tightened around me, and we walked to a small bar in the corner where we ordered more bubbly.

I leaned against the bar for support and realized perspiration was running down my temples.

I was woozy from the warm room, my heady voyeurism, and the promise of oh so many things...

CHAPTER 28

BRODIE

One of the hottest things I'd ever seen was the gorgeous Nara Kincaid walking around a sex club, taking it all in and loving it.

And I wasn't the only one enjoying watching her. She'd been turning heads since she'd arrived. I was impatient for the moment I could run my lips over every inch of her body, but I was following her lead.

If she wasn't completely comfortable, it wasn't going to be fun for either of us.

We've all had sex, sure, and some of us have had a shit ton, like I have. But a setting where people are having sex out in the open, where you could put on a little show yourself—that was something different altogether.

It brought sensuality to an entirely other level if you were up for it.

And, it seemed Nara was.

"You doing okay?" I asked her.

"Yeah," she said breathlessly, continuing to look around with heavy-lidded eyes.

We hadn't started anything, and already her nipples were rock hard and her lips engorged, begging to be kissed.

Being the nice guy that I was, I obliged by gently backing her against a wall and brushing my lips over hers.

"You know how hot it makes me to see you watching all this fucking? And knowing you're loving it?" I asked.

Her breath hitched. I'd nailed what was running through her head probably better than she would have been able to.

"And I'm hard, baby," I told her.

Damn if her fine hand didn't reach down and grab my cock through my trousers.

Her head fell back against the wall, eyes closed, while I moved my kisses to her bare throat.

Slowly—in case she wanted to stop me—I began to undress her right there in view of the whole club. It was all I could do not to whip out my cock and start stroking it.

"Brodie," she whispered.

I put my hands on either side of her face. "Yeah?"

"I want to…" She licked her lips.

"What, baby?" I whispered in her ear.

"Let's get naked," she murmured. Her eyes reopened, focusing on an unoccupied sofa on the other side of the room. She took my hand and led me to it.

I sat while she stood in front of me, swaying to the slow, sexy background music. I put my hands on her hips, and she placed hers over mine. She looked like a goddess with her hair swinging over her unbuttoned blouse.

I unzipped her skirt and pulled it down over her hips, and she was left wearing only a tiny silk thong. I clutched her ass cheeks and pulled close enough to smell her sweet pussy.

I pushed the blouse off her shoulders and took a quick look around catching the admiring glances of other guests, both male and female.

She reached to unhook her bra, letting it fall to the floor, and in a swift movement slid her thong down her legs and stepped out of the tangle of clothing that had puddled at her feet. She stood before me in nothing but her shoes.

Holy mother of god.

Her skin was silky and heated. If I hadn't known better, I would have sworn she had a fever. But it was just the headiness of the club. As I reached to caress her breasts, she took a step toward me.

Raising one foot onto the sofa next to me, she spread her legs enough to give me perfect access to her beautiful pussy, like a gift.

I slid my tongue into her pretty slit, and she shivered hard, her head dropping back. Just below the tiny triangle of hair on her mound, I spread her open to find her glistening and erect clit, which I flicked with my tongue.

She found purchase by gripping my hair. This was a ride that she was ready to go on.

I burrowed my tongue, my fingers opening her more, and she tilted her hips to increase the pleasure. I wanted to devour her whole, but forced myself to slow.

I skimmed two fingers along the length of her swollen lips, up and back and she rocked on my hand, moaning. She gripped my hair harder, and when I looked up for a moment I found her trembling.

She was close, and I needed to give her everything she craved.

I set to work, fingers banging her pussy, my lips closed over her clit. Her hips thrust in time to my pumping. In seconds, she stiffened. Her pussy throbbed around my hand as she reached her orgasm moaning, all breathy and sweet, with pleading noises escaping her parted lips.

She collapsed on the sofa next to me as she took one of my fingers to taste herself, unselfconscious about our surroundings.

"You were so wet, baby," I murmured, kissing her.

"Brodie?"

"Yes, baby?"

"Do we still have the condoms they gave us at the front door?"

"Right here," I said, producing one.

She took it from my hand, and freed me from my trousers. She carefully rolled it down over my cock, which was now begging to explode.

She straddled me on the sofa, lowering herself to rub my head on her sensitive clit. I grasped my cock and looked up at her.

"Ready, baby?" I asked.

"Yeah," she breathed, and lowered herself until she engulfed my head.

Gasping, she dropped further until she stretched to accommodate me. I was buried to my balls, my hands on her ass cheeks, letting her take the lead. From her position above me, she had perfect leverage and ground herself on me until her pussy clenched again.

"I…I'm coming…" she murmured weakly.

That was it. I was done. I couldn't hold on any longer and exploded in her tight, wet heat with a groan that turned at least a few heads.

I held her hips and pounded her, thrusting my cock up and down inside her. We were lost in a manic craving for release and blood roared through my ears as I called her name.

I was left shuddering violently, sweaty, out of breath, and amazed that I had somehow found her.

CHAPTER 29

NARA

I barely remember leaving the club or getting home.

When I woke up the next day in Brodie's loft everything was sunny and white, like I was in heaven.

Come to think of it, I definitely had been the previous night when Brodie and I had not only fucked with a fury I'd never thought was possible, but in a public place, too.

I had no idea what had come over me there, but the atmosphere of open sex had been a powerful aphrodisiac. It was so massively empowering. I couldn't really even think.

All I knew was I wanted Brodie inside me.

Pushing myself up in bed, I realized his side was empty. I got up and peeked over the loft railing. Below, he was having what sounded like a business conversation.

"I mean, yeah. If the investors wanted me in San Francisco, I wouldn't be opposed to moving there. I love the place. And I have faith that my general manager here in

New York could keep things moving forward. It would take me a couple weeks to close up things here, but I could be out there pretty quickly..."

Holy shit? He was leaving New York? And he hadn't even told me.

Never even mentioned it.

I found my clothes and pulled them on as fast as I could. They were wrinkly from having been stepped all over the night before, but I had no time to go home to change. I had to get to the office to iron out the last of our software issues before our next beta meeting. And I wanted to get the hell out of Brodie's bed—fast.

Good thing I wore pretty much the same thing every day. No one would know any different.

I heard Brodie coming up the steps to the bedroom, so I ducked into the bathroom where I found a new toothbrush and tidied up. Luckily, I kept a makeup collection at the office, so I could pretty well hide up the fact that I was doing a major walk of shame.

"'Morning, baby. How'd you sleep?" he hollered through the door.

I could hear him riffling through his closet, no doubt planning the day's master of the universe outfit.

What was up with freaking moving to San Francisco?

But I wasn't going to ask. If he wasn't going to volunteer that he was about to hightail it out of town, I wasn't going to be the neurotic chick who gave him shit about it.

Who cared anyway? I'd only been on a few dates with him. It wouldn't be the first time someone bailed on me after I put out. I rushed out of the bathroom to avoid conversation. Grabbing my shoes, I ran down the stairs.

Brodie called after me, "Hey, where's the fire? Nara? Can I have the limo take you home?"

"No," I called up the stairs. I leaned against the wall to pull on my pumps. "I'll grab a cab. Talk to you later."

I let his heavy apartment door slam behind me and hustled down the hall as fast as my heels would let me. As luck would have it, a cab was passing by that I jumped into before Brodie could follow me to see what the hell was up.

If he couldn't figure it out, to hell with him.

By the time I arrived at work, my mood had gone from crappy to all out horrendous. How could he not have told me he was leaving town? Jesus, I was an idiot.

"Nara," Mimi called as I whizzed past her. "Coffee?"

"Thanks, Mimi. That would be great."

I must have looked like shit, because her eyes widened ever so slightly when I turned to her. Makeup drawer, here I come.

I listened to my voicemail messages while I put my face on. The first was from Becca.

"Nara, sweetie, your mom says you're not coming back for the reunion. Is that true? I'm so bummed. *Everyone* is just dying to see you."

Right. Everyone was just dying to see the class slut. I didn't think so.

The next message was from my mom.

"Well, Nara, you've succeeded in disappointing a lot of people with your stubborn refusal to come home. I just don't understand it. It's not like you had a horrible childhood or anything like that."

Had I had a horrible childhood? Probably not. But a Norman Rockwell childhood it hadn't been, either.

The last message was from Simon.

"Nara, I've been thinking about what you said. I'd like to talk."

Oh. My. God.

Had we broken past our standoff? Might I finally be rid of him?

Joi popped in and handed me a coffee. "Here you go. Mimi asked me to bring this back. She seemed kind of afraid of you this morning."

Note to self—apologize to Mimi later. And call the creepy faux husband back.

"Yeah, I arrived in a fury. I'm fine, though." I forced a smile.

"Mmmm. You don't look fine." She leaned onto my desk. "I know you. I know when you're fine, and I know when you're not. Spill it."

Ugh. She was right. I was horrible at hiding my moods, especially from her.

"Well, I spent last night with Brodie."

Her face lit up with the kind of excitement usually saved for winners of the lottery. The *big* lottery.

"Ooooh, was it hot?"

If she only knew…

"It was great," I said, nodding. "Until I woke up this morning to hear him talking about moving to San Francisco. Apparently, it's supposed to happen very soon."

I caught the hitch in my throat before Joi heard it.

"He's moving and didn't tell you?" she asked with raised eyebrows.

"Correct. Apparently, he's leaving town. Never bothered telling me. Nice guy, huh?" I slammed my desk drawer so hard my pencil cup went crashing off my desk.

There went my Mommy Knows mug, smashed to bits.

"Maybe there's some kind of misunderstanding?" she asked hopefully.

After picking up the shards of my mug, I huffed back to my chair. With nowhere to put my pens, I just dropped them on top of my desk where they landed like Pickup Stix.

"I don't know. I don't care. I'm just done. Done, done, done." I buried my face in my hands.

Joi jumped up and put her arm around me. "Okay. I'm sorry, sweetie. This just sucks. Hey, look at me."

I took my hands off my face. "Yeah?"

"We have a big day ahead. Let's focus, and afterward, we'll go out for a nice dinner."

I nodded slowly. I needed a damn vacation. Maybe I should have planned to go back for my reunion.

No wait, scratch that.

That was the last thing I needed—to feel like even more of a freak than I did when growing up there.

We got to work on the last of our testing. We had to make sure our app could confidently tell the difference between number one and number two.

Such a glamorous life I led.

CHAPTER 30

BRODIE

Nara had run out of my place like her pants were on fire.

Strange, because she never seemed to worry much about being late before. Clearly, something was up, but she had split so fast I couldn't ask what was eating at her. Maybe she hadn't liked the club after all? Had I pressured her to go? God, I hoped not.

I'd get to the bottom of it. First, though, I had to get to work.

I started by calling my lawyer. "Joe, Brodie here," I said.

"Hey there. Hope all is well."

"All is well, and I think it's about to get better. Go ahead and send the buy-out papers to Wooten's and Evershire's attorneys. I'll call them in a little while. We'll see what they say, and I'll leave the door open for a counter offer. I suspect they'll be surprised as hell."

"Got it. What else?" Joe asked.

"Next, my brother in San Francisco has rounded up a group of investors to open a sister hotel there."

"Wow. That's amazing news."

"It is. I'm psyched. Can you draw up partnership papers for this? I'll email you all the pertinent info. And one last thing."

"Yes?"

"I'm moving to San Francisco."

"Oh, you lucky bastard. I love that city."

"I do, too. I have some things to wrap up here, but the New York hotel will be in good hands with my general manager. And I'll be back and forth all the time."

"So now you'll be breaking hearts on the West Coast. I guess you ran out of women here in New York?" He laughed.

"It's funny, but the shoe is on the other foot these days. I'm the one who may end up with the broken heart."

Next, I got my partners on the phone. I suspected they'd be shocked as hell when they found out HWE Enterprises was about to drop the W and the E. That is, if all went according to plan.

"Brodie," one of them said, "to what do we owe this honor?"

"Hey, guys."

I didn't want to hate them, especially since my father essentially stole money from their fathers. But because of all that went down, I was pretty sure they hated me. Or at least resented me. To be honest, couldn't say I blamed them.

"I have a proposition for you," I started.

"Brodie," one of them interrupted, "we've already told

you we're not interested in the San Francisco expansion—"

"That's not what I'm calling about, guys," I interrupted. Might was well try to keep it friendly.

I got to the point. "I'm prepared to buy you out of HWE. To release you of the partnership by paying a lump sum balance of what you're owed."

"Well, Brodie, no need to be so rash—"

"This isn't rash at all, Steve. I've given this a lot of thought, and I think what I'm offering is more than fair. It covers what's owed to you in damages due to my father's actions."

"Um…well…I don't—" one of them said.

"Look, guys. I'm going to be straight with you. I know you've wanted to get rid of me. I don't know why, since it was *my* hard work that turned Hotel Vertigo into what it is today. But I know you wanted to buy me out. And now I want to buy you out."

"Well, Brodie, we're not really interested in an offer like that—" one of them said.

"Wait," the other chimed in, "What *is* the offer?"

Now I had them where I wanted them.

"My lawyer is sending over the papers within the hour. I think you'll find them more than generous."

I ended the call. My plan of catching them unaware worked perfectly. It would take them some time to digest all I'd said, but by the time they got my offer packet, the pump would be primed. Honestly, it was an offer they couldn't refuse.

Wow. Moving to San Francisco. It was a long way from New York, but I was ready for a change and to see my brother on a more regular basis. I wondered, however, if it would be far enough to escape the guilt of my father's sins…?

Now to see if Nara wanted to be part of my plan.

I hoped to god she did.

CHAPTER 31

NARA

The day flew, and by the end of it, my mood had upgraded from crappy to hopeful but resigned.

The Mommy Knows software sensors were working like the champs I knew they were, and that was a huge load off everyone's back.

The moms who had come in for the day's test had raved about the results, thrilled that they might be able to know their little ones had a dirty diaper practically before the kid did.

I'd left Simon two messages but strangely had not heard back. I was hoping against hope we'd reached some sort of détente, and that I would get my divorce with no further trouble.

But who was I kidding?

And I'd pretty much convinced myself to just let the whole Brodie thing go. He was just one guy, like many others, who'd come into my life. And then out of it. I'd had some fun with him, and I'd forget about him in due time. No harm, no foul.

And yet...

No. I would not waste my time thinking about how he touched me and was so in tune with me that a single look made me weak in the knees. And then there were those dark eyes that looked at me like he saw every bit of who I was.

Yeah, right. Forget it.

I straightened up my desk and headed to Joi's cubicle.

"Well, look who left her laptop on her desk," she said, observing my lack of tote bag.

I nodded. "Yup. I'm leaving it here. We're going out, and I'd like to try and forget about work for one evening. Just one."

She stood up and grabbed her things. "I'm with ya on that, sweetie. Let's roll."

We headed out the door like we had serious business to take care of. And we did.

Five minutes later, Joi and I settled into a dark paneled place staffed by hipster bartenders with man buns, retro mustaches, and bow ties.

"What'll you have?" she asked me.

"Scotch. On the rocks."

"Damn. Goin for the hard stuff. All righty then, I'll join ya," she said.

The first sip of the brown liquor burned the hell out of my throat and reminded me why I hardly ever drank the stuff. And of course, it reminded me of Brodie.

Big mistake.

"So what's the latest with the wedding?" I asked.

Talking about it thrilled her to no end, and I was happy to oblige. I could sip my burning scotch, toss back a few of the salty peanuts they'd set before us, and smile and nod. The problem with that, though, was that my mind wandered back to exactly where I didn't want it.

Joi's elbow stuck in my side. "Are you listening?"

I perked up. "Yeah. Of course."

Hand on hip, she asked, "Okay then, what was I just saying?"

"Something about purple tablecloths and white flowers?" Not my taste but whatever.

"No. No, that is not what I was talking about. I said we'd decided on *white* tablecloths and *purple* flowers," she said with great offense.

"I'm sorry, sweetie. I'm distracted. You busted me." I shook my head.

Ugh.

Joi put her hand on my arm. "Okay, hotel guy is moving across the country. What are you gonna do about it?"

"Huh? There's nothing *to* do about it. He doesn't even know I know. Apparently, he didn't care enough to mention it to me." I swallowed the lump in my throat. I was not going to cry over that jerk.

"Look," Joi said, "you want my opinion?"

Not really. "Okay."

"You don't have the whole story. I know you don't like me telling you this, but I've seen you jump to conclusions before. You drive yourself crazy. You drive *me* crazy."

I shrugged. "Yeah. That's me." I took another sip of my scotch. It wasn't burning nearly as badly now.

The phone rattled in my pocket.

Guess who?

we need to talk. are you free?

I put my phone face down on the bar. Time to change the subject.

"So the tests went well today, didn't they?"

"What? Oh yeah." She nodded. "Pretty exciting. Now that our proof of concept is solid, do you think the investors will come through? I mean, with some nice, green cash?"

"Ugh, I hope so."

I hadn't been working on this damn software application every day of my life for the last several years for it to go nowhere.

My phone vibrated again, skittering a few inches across the bar.

I picked it up and yes, it was him again. A knot in my stomach tightened.

"Who is it?" Joi asked, craning to see my phone screen. "Oh, it's him! Answer it!"

I turned my phone away from her. "Do you mind? This is personal."

i'm serious. i need to see u.

Joi threw her hands up in the air. "He has no idea you are tweaked at him. At least give him a chance."

i'm out with joi.

where can I meet you?

why do you want to meet?

c'mon. it's important.

all right. come meet us at epic grill.

c u in 20.

I put my phone down. "He's on his way here."

"Thatta girl! Talk it out. I'm sure everything will make sense soon."

A huge grin was plastered over her face as if she'd won the lottery.

She kind of *had* won the lottery. Unlike me.

Brodie entered the bar like he'd been born in the place. That's how confident he was, never looking out of place, never facing a moment of faltering confidence.

What must that be like?

I watched him over Joi's shoulder as he scanned the bar, looking for us. When his gaze met mine, my heart nearly pounded out of my chest. *Damn him.*

"Ladies," he said with a quick peck on my lips. He shook Joi's hand, leaving her beaming like she'd solved the world's problems.

"Brodie! So nice to meet you," she gushed.

That was the effect he had on women.

He took a sip of my drink and raised his eyebrows. "Whoa. Going for the hard stuff."

When I tore my gaze from his magnificent face, I saw Joi gathering her things.

"You guys. I am just exhausted," she said with great drama. "And I have another early day tomorrow."

She gave Brodie a squeeze on the arm, which she clearly enjoyed, and leaned to hug me.

"Don't be a bitch," she whispered in my ear.

I made a silent plan to kill her first chance I got.

"Good night all!" she sang as she sauntered out of the bar.

That left just Brodie and me, staring at each other. He climbed into Joi's vacated bar stool and shook the ice cubes in her half-drunk scotch.

"So," he started, "what was with the quick exit this morning?"

He didn't waste any time, did he?

I shrugged one shoulder. "Big day. Yeah, I had a big day. In fact, our testing went really well today—"

He held his hand up to stop me.

"No. That's not why you left." He looked serious. "I need you to be honest."

Well, shit.

If he wanted honesty, he was going to get honesty.

I took a sip of my drink and straightened my back. "I overheard you planning your move to San Francisco."

I looked at the ice melting in my drink, leaving wavy lines as it mixed with the booze.

He ran his fingers through his hair and sighed loudly. "So you just leave? Without a word?"

I chewed on my bottom lip. "What was there to say? I heard all I needed to."

He looked up at the ceiling as if he were counting to three. Then he turned on his barstool to face me directly. "I'm sorry."

I shrugged. The sooner this ended, the better.

He continued. "I'm sorry you heard only part of the story."

"What else is there to know?" I asked.

"That I want you to come with me. To San Francisco."

CHAPTER 32

BRODIE

So that's why she'd hightailed it out of my place that morning. Thank god I'd chased her down and gotten to the bottom of her silent treatment.

I don't know what she did to me, but I was just wrecked by her. Nothing was as important as it had been before. Not the hotel, not my dad's misdeeds, not my business partners. Nothing.

And you know what?

It felt damn good.

There was a clarity in everything that I'd never had before. Like a fog had lifted, and I knew how to get where I was supposed to go. It narrowed my focus, and for a change, I knew exactly where I should be heading.

Nara. It was Nara.

"So, will you come with me to San Francisco?" I repeated.

She looked at me like I was crazy. Which was to be expected.

She crinkled her nose. "What? No. I can't move to San Francisco. But I wish you well there."

Clearly, my work wasn't done. Not that I'd expected it to be a slam-dunk.

"Why?" I asked.

"Why what?"

"Why can't you come to San Francisco with me?"

She rolled her eyes. "Well, for one, I have a company here. A company that is about to take off."

She had a point. But I'd thought that through.

"Okay. Why else?" I asked.

"Because…my life is here. I don't want to leave New York." She was shredding the bar napkin in her hands.

"Anything else?" I asked.

"I barely know you. And you barely know me."

She had me on that one. And she was absolutely right.

I put my finger under her chin and turned her face toward mine. Very slowly, I lowered my lips to hers, barely touching them. Drawing back, I could see her eyes had fluttered closed, her lips relaxed and receptive.

So I dove in to seal the deal.

I returned to her mouth, devouring her lips until she gasped for breath. I didn't care that we were in public. If anyone had anything to say, they could just fuck off.

"Brodie," she whispered.

"What, baby?" I pressed my forehead to hers and inhaled her clean hair. God, I loved that smell.

I looked at her beautiful face, framed by masses of

dark waves, her red lipstick smudged thanks to my hungry kiss. A single tear ran down her cheek.

I threw some money on the bar and grabbed her hand. "C'mon. Let's go."

We jumped into the limo. This time, I closed the window *and* privacy screen separating us from the driver. I wasn't going to share this woman with anyone, much less a chauffeur.

Nara grabbed at my trousers to free my stiff cock from a tangle of shirttails and boxers.

When her hand reached my sensitive flesh, I grit my teeth to keep from exploding right then. Her touch drove shock waves to the ends of my limbs, and I convulsed with its power.

Before I knew it, she'd engulfed my entire cock with her sweet mouth, taking me until I banged against the back of her throat. I don't know how she did it, but it was fucking amazing.

One of her warms hands found my balls and Christ, I nearly shot right then and there. But I had to hold off. I wanted her pussy.

As if she read my mind, she reached under her skirt, removing her panties. She dug in her purse and pulled out one of the condoms we'd gotten at the club the night before.

I took it from her, knowing I could get it on my dick faster, and she positioned herself right over me, her hair falling in my face. I reached for her soaked pussy and opened her to allow my entrance.

I gave her a couple inches, watching for her reaction.

She grimaced slightly, letting me know to slow down. I waited for her to relax and open, and for her take control.

Swaying with the motion of the moving car, she rocked her hips lower a little at a time until I was balls-deep inside her.

I unbuttoned her blouse, the same one from the night before, and released her breasts to my hungry mouth. I sucked her nipples until she gasped, and she ground harder on my dick.

"God, Brodie," she murmured.

"Yeah? Yeah, baby?"

"Fuck me. I'm coming," she breathed.

I grabbed her delicious hips and pistoned her on my cock, up and down until she screamed in orgasm. She threw her head back, half-moaning, half-laughing as she pressed her tits into my face.

A moment later, my balls tightened and my own eruption ran up my dick and into her clenching pussy. I threw my head back, banging it on the car seatback to release the tension that had built in every fiber of my muscles.

Holy shit.

"Baby?" I whispered in her ear.

"Yeah?" she asked weakly.

"You better fucking come to California with me."

CHAPTER 33 & OTHER STUFF

NARA

In confronting Brodie about his plans to take off for San Francisco, I'd gotten myself an invite.

Well, I guess the invite had been part of his plan all along.

But still.

He was crazy to think I'd just up and move. I barely freaking knew him, for one. And yet, he somehow knew I'd say yes. That took a supreme amount of arrogance on his part.

But since I'd met him at that silly fundraising auction all sorts of things had taken an interesting turn.

After weeks of flying back and forth across the country to wear me down, Brodie had convinced me to agree to visit the city with him. Just visit.

And so far, it was fabulous.

From our hotel room in the Fairmont on Nob Hill, the foghorns blared low and loud. It was no wonder they could be heard clear across the city. In the week since we'd been in San Francisco, it seemed like they never stopped.

And I loved them more than I could describe.

Then there was the clanging of the cable cars. From our hotel, we had a perfect view of the California Street line when it passed by laden with tourists and the occasional commuter. It was a charmingly quaint reminder of a brilliant, modern city's past.

I'd taken to getting up at five thirty every morning so I could be on the same schedule as my team back in New York.

Working remotely had gone pretty well so far. In fact, it hadn't even seemed like I *was* remote. Everything was pretty much the same except that I dialed into meetings I used to hold in person.

After things had calmed down from Joi's wedding, she dove into running the office, and things there were perking along with better efficiency than I'd ever managed.

The top venture capital firm in the country had decided to back Mommy Knows. It was an incredible rush to realize such heavy hitters believed in our work. And the mommies were loving us and their new method for baby hygiene.

Mimi had thought of that tag line—*baby hygiene.*

My phone rang, the screen reading *Mom.*

"Hey, Mom."

She was still tweaked I'd not come back for my reunion. I suspected no one else had really noticed. Well, except for Becca.

"Sweetie. How is everything in sunny California?"

"Great, Mom. Except it's really not sunny in San Francisco. It's mostly foggy."

"Oh, you are so funny. Everyone knows it's sunny in California. Are you just trying to keep me away?"

I held the phone away so she couldn't hear me sigh. "Mom, you know Brodie and I would love for you to visit."

"Well, I don't want to impose. How long do you plan to be there?"

That was a good question.

"Not sure yet, Mom. You want to come next week?"

"Well, are you sure that's okay with Brodie?" She didn't care whether it was okay with me.

"Yes, Mom."

Brodie's new Hotel Vertigo West, in the city's up-and-coming Tenderloin district, had come together at lightning speed.

I guess that's how things went when you had the budget you needed and knew what you were doing. In fact, a giant opening party was scheduled for later that evening.

He'd been working so much I'd hardly seen him, but what I had seen impressed the hell out of me. The man really knew how to take care of business, having gotten the place up and running in no time.

And he still kept an eye on the New York property

after he'd successfully jettisoned his hostile business partners.

My Skype rang, and I answered a video call from Joi. If it was possible, she'd grown even more beautiful since she'd gotten married.

"Hey," she said.

"Hey. You look great. I love your hair," I told her.

"Really? Supposedly, this long bob is all the rage right now. They're calling it a *lob*." She fingered it as if she still wasn't quite sure she'd done the right thing with a big chop.

"Anyway," she continued, "I'm calling because some official-looking papers just arrived for you. Want me to open them?"

"Yes, please. I'm still waiting on that stuff from Simon."

She tore open a large envelope in view of my screen and sorted through a couple sheets.

"Wow. Congrats. Looks like you are finally officially divorced."

Oh. My. God.

I'd been waiting so long to hear those words.

I was through. Through with my fake marriage and through with that little peckerhead, Simon, and his terrible betrayal. He'd oddly gone dark after my last message from him. A couple weeks later I'd found out he'd been deported, his INS fraud having been "anony-mously" reported.

I didn't know who ratted him out, and I didn't want to. But I had my suspicions.

"Wow. It's finally done," I said.

Joi nodded and shook a finger at me through my computer screen.

"No more fake marriages."

I laughed. "Absolutely. One fake marriage almost did me in."

Brodie came over to kiss me good bye just before eight a.m., the time he usually went to work. I was in my corner of our hotel suite, working away.

"I'll see you later to pick you up for tonight's party?" he asked.

"Yeah, babe. I think it will be a good one." Supposedly everyone who was anyone in San Francisco would be there, and I was looking forward to meeting some new people. Additionally, we'd hired an incredibly inventive caterer. I couldn't wait to pig out.

"What are you going to wear?" Brodie asked.

I had hoped he'd ask that. "Not sure yet. Why?"

He shrugged. "I was hoping you'd wear that slinky white number I got you awhile back."

"Oh, that," I said.

"What's wrong with that one? You were drop dead gorgeous in it."

"Thank you. I did feel pretty good in it. But it doesn't fit anymore."

"What? What do you mean?" he asked.

"Well, it fits, just not that well."

"Are you serious? Well, that's a bummer." He walked

up behind me and started in with one of his amazing shoulder massages.

"Yeah. I mean, it's kind of a bummer. But it's to be expected."

"Why? All the good California food we've been eating?" he asked.

"Well, part of it is the food."

"The great wine, too, huh?" He patted his incredibly flat stomach. "I think I need to cut back a little, myself."

"No, you're fine. It's me we have to watch out for."

The color drained from his face.

"Is something wrong?" He crouched before me and took my hands.

"Nothing is wrong. Nothing at all. But I think I'll need to go shopping for new clothes soon."

"Well, I think you are more beautiful than ever. California looks good on you, my Miss Happy." He stood and kissed the top of my head, returning to his closet to finish dressing.

"How do you think a baby would look on me?" My heart pounded.

He stopped what he was doing and whipped around. "What? Huh?"

"Well, there's a reason my clothes don't fit, and that I'll have to go shopping soon."

His head tilted. Poor guy looked so confused.

I couldn't mess with him any longer.

"I'm pregnant. We're gonna have a baby," I said, rubbing the tiny swell in my belly that he hadn't noticed.

Please let him be okay with the news.

His eyes bugged, and his mouth dropped open. My master of the universe was speechless.

All because of a little baby.

Tears sprang to his eyes. He ran over and crouched before me again, taking my hands in his shaking ones.

"Please tell me you're serious," he begged. "Please."

"I take it you want a little Nara or Brodie, then?" I asked.

Now, I was choking up.

"Holy fucking shit, *yes*," he shouted. "And since all that fake marriage stuff is behind you, you might want to consider marrying me." He threw his head back and laughed the happiest laugh I'd ever heard.

"I'll think about it..." I teased.

He pulled me out of my chair and spun me around. "God, I love you Nara Kincaid. Will you marry me?"

"I think I will. But first, I'll want to check your citizenship status. No more green card weddings for me."

~

Get a free short story!
Join my Insider Group

~

If you liked *Sinful Little Betrayal*, check out this excerpt from:
Mister Hollywood
An Escort Romance, Book 1

Chapter 1
Belle

The pink fabric strained—I honestly didn't know how it didn't completely rupture—across what looked like two giant balloons. But they weren't balloons. They were two of the biggest freaking boobs I'd ever seen.

I didn't normally spend much time looking at other women's boobs. After all, I had my own. And while they were nothing to write home about, when I checked them out in the mirror at home they were nice enough, if on the small side. No complaints on my part.

"They're...nice, Jackie," I said to my best friend at work. Actually, she was my best friend, period.

She looked down on her protuberant chest, nodding in happy appreciation of my compliment. As if she, or anyone else, could miss the enhancements. Could she actually see her feet over those massive new mounds of silicone?

"Aren't they great? I am soooo freaking thrilled with my new girls." She cupped them and they poured over the tops of her hands.

I looked around the car dealership, where I was the receptionist and all-round office gopher bitch. From the other side of the showroom, where he sat overlooking our every move, our boss, Ted, caught Jackie feeling herself up. He frowned for a moment, shook his head, and went back to the paperwork on his desk.

The poor man tried to keep all of us in line, but his efforts were usually futile. Car salesmen and women are typically a bit on the crazy side, although that didn't begin to explain Jackie's eccentricities. But when you're top salesperson by a factor of five, you could pretty much do whatever the hell you wanted to at work.

And Jackie clearly wanted to keep talking about her new boobs. I could deal with that—after all, she was that good of a friend.

"Hold on a sec, would you?" I asked, as I picked up a call and directed it to our service department.

I returned my attention to Jackie and her new boobs. "So. How are you feeling? All the stitches gone?"

She leaned closer to me, as if she were all of sudden going for privacy. "Not yet. The doctor said he wants to make sure there's as little scarring as possible. I need to keep them bound up for a bit longer. So, no test-driving yet, but I can't wait to try them out on some lucky guy. It'll be so freaking hot."

Breaking off our conversation, she scanned the show-room like a shark looking for her next meal. "Gotta go!" she said, thrusting her chest out and making for a couple bickering over a red convertible.

Jackie was like a shrink for people looking for cars. The car-whisperer, I called her. Somehow, she got the most belligerent folks to calm down, listen to her, trust her, and then of course, buy from her. That's how she came to be so loaded.

Not that I begrudged the woman anything. Lord, no. She worked her ass off, and she was generous, to boot. I mean, she had twins at home whose dad did not pay a cent in child support. Obviously, she had to make things happen. And, god bless her, more often than not she paid for me, too, like when we had a girls' nights out.

So I got back to the phones and my other glamorous responsibilities like checking on the clogged toilet in the women's room. I also directed a new customer to Starla, Jackie's archrival in both the boob and sales category. At one time, Starla had been the lead salesperson, powered by a breathy voice, big blue eyes, and an ass that was almost certainly surgically enhanced. But when Jackie came to town, she stole the honor right from under her so fast that everyone's heads at the dealership had spun. And Starla had pretty much hated Jackie ever since. The rivalry was epic.

At noon on the dot, Jackie headed my way for lunch.

"Usual place?" I asked after I hung up, grabbing my purse.

"Of course. Let's go." Jackie said, leading me to her custom-painted gold-tone Mercedes.

That's how she rolled.

The smell of a House of Waffles sort of restaurant had always done something to me. Maybe it was going there as a kid, or maybe it was the comfort of late-night drunken meals in college, when I'd earned my useless art degree. Whatever it was, we'd no sooner walked in and I was instantly in my happy place. How was it that a smell from the past could be so damn good?

And even though House of Waffles specialized in breakfast foods, they had so much more, including an amazing Monte Cristo sandwich I ordered every single time I went there. That day was no exception.

"Hey, ladies. Good to see you. The usual?" our regular waitress asked.

Jackie looked at me and rolled her eyes. "You're getting the same damn thing as always, aren't you?"

The waitress laughed, scribbling on her order pad. "Don't give the girl a hard time. She knows what she likes. What'll you have, Jackie?"

"Ummm…" Jackie said, flipping through the menu, as if she didn't know by heart everything they served there. As much as she gave me a hard time for ordering the same thing all the time, she did the same thing, herself.

"I'll have the Greek salad," she finally said as she handed her menu back to the waitress. As if there really were a decision to be made.

The waitress clicked her pen and nodded." All righty, ladies. Be right back with your ice teas."

"So how are ya?" Jackie asked from across the booth, where her newly acquired breasts nearly rested on the tabletop.

I shrugged. "Good, I guess. Why?"

"Eh. I don't know," Jackie said with an inquisitive look. "I thought you looked a bit frazzled this morning. Did your classes already start up?"

Did I look that bad?

"No. I haven't enrolled for this semester yet. Classes start in a couple weeks. I gotta decide what I'm doing about continuing in accounting or not."

"What are you waiting for?" she asked.

Lowering my voice, I leaned toward her and looked out the window to the parking lot.

"I guess I'm feeling a bit of a setback. And it's actually

been a huge distraction." I saw a familiar car slowly pass by, and the temperature dropped twenty degrees inside me.

"Don't beat yourself up, sweetie," Jackie said, her eyes glancing out the window but not seeing what I saw. "You've been through some shit. Do you think he's still looking for you?"

I shivered in the overheated restaurant as thoughts of my asshole ex-husband threatened to ruin my lunch.

"I want to believe he's not looking and that's he finally forgotten about me, but I'm not sure I'll ever get there. I could have sworn I saw his car the other day. I started shaking and froze right there in place. I need to be more resilient. Tougher. You know what I mean?"

Our food came, and I dove into my sandwich. At least I still had my appetite.

"Well, I'm sure you're just being paranoid. He'll never find you here. L.A.'s too big." Jackie watched a splotch of salad dressing land on her bosom, leaving an oily stain right on top of the girls. One of the downsides of having big ones?

I took a deep breath and looked at her, hoping to god she was right. I *needed* her to be right.

"So, that's what's been weighing on me. Now you know," I told her, deciding it was time to change the subject. "Hey, did I tell you the cutest guy came into the dealership the other day? He was so nice, chatting me up and all. Then Starla swept in and dragged him away."

"Ugh. She's such a whore."

The rivalry to end all others. I never should have brought her name up. No good would come of it.

And true to my fears, Jackie strung together a barrage of swear words that aptly conveyed her contempt for Starla. I got it—it was pretty much unheard of for a busy car dealership to have *one* top-selling woman, but to have *two* was freakishly uncommon. And those two went at it like pissed-off alley cats when the customers weren't around. The story was that when Jackie joined the company and started giving Starla a run for her money, all bets were off. Bigger screaming matches had never been seen or heard. Apparently the worst of it had been put to rest long before I'd joined the company—but their disdain for each other was barely concealed.

"Hey, we'd better get back," I said, checking the clock on the wall. "I don't want Ted yelling at me for being late. Again."

"That old windbag can suck my dick," Jackie said as she pulled out a twenty to cover our bill. She always paid at House of Waffles. I'd offer to pitch in or leave the tip, but she wouldn't allow me to. Like I could ever pay her back for all she'd done for me. Not in this lifetime.

Having something in common like abusive ex-husbands, as Jackie and I did, builds a serious bond between friends. We'd been thick as thieves ever since we learned each other's stories, and seriously had each other's backs.

She hooked her arm through mine as we walked back to her Mercedes.

"Ya know what, sweetie? I think you need a little nookie."

No shit. "I *know* I need a little nookie. Actually more

than a little. But dontcha think I have bigger fish to fry at this point?"

Ignoring my prudence, she continued. "I may have an idea for you."

No, no, no. Jackie saying 'I may have an idea' was akin to someone saying 'hold my beer.' Disaster was usually the result.

"Jackie, I know all about your ideas. Thanks, but no thanks."

"Just give me a chance, Belle. You gotta trust me."

I smiled out the window. "You know what happened last time I trusted you."

"Hey, it wasn't my fault the guy used a fake picture on his profile," Jackie pleaded. "But he *did* pay for your drinks. So there's that."

I gave her the best stink eye I could muster.

"Miss Belle," Ted boomed.

Why was he hanging out behind the reception desk? *My* reception desk?

A quick look at my watch told me I was returning right on time. Not that it mattered. My backups in the service department always covered for me if I were late. 'Course, I did the same for them.

"Hi, Ted." I put on my headset and punched a few numbers on the phone console.

"Belle," he started, staring straight down at me in my chair.

Why did he have to be such a douchebag?

"I have a bone to pick with you," he continued.

Yeah, no shit, Sherlock.

"What's up, Ted? Is something the matter?" I asked with my best fake-pleasant voice.

"You didn't get me a very important phone message," he said in that imperious 'I'm the boss and I'm always correct' voice he used far too often.

"What? Are you sure?"

"Yes. A Mr. Reid called for me this morning. He's one of our best customers. Buys a new car for himself and nearly everyone in his family every year. He called me back just a few minutes ago, furious I'd not gotten back to him."

I turned to my computer and typed maniacally. I always entered online the messages I took and forwarded them to whoever was supposed to get them.

"There, Ted. Right there." I pointed at my screen that proved I had indeed sent him his message.

"Where? I don't see it. Where is it?" he asked, squinting through his glasses.

Dude needed to get his vision checked.

"Right there," I said, pressing my finger on the computer screen so he couldn't miss it.

"Oh," he said, snapping back up to his full height. "Well then."

Ah, the sweet taste of victory. "Is there anything else I can help you with, Ted?"

"No, Belle. There is not." He hurried back to his desk like his pants were on fire, while I just watched, shaking my head.

Christ, with men like him all over my ass, no wonder

I'd not gone on a date in a year. Or had it been even longer?

And as if Ted's admonishment hadn't been humiliating enough, Starla happened by my desk.

"Hey'ya, Stella-Bella."

She thought we were good enough friends that she could nickname me.

"What's up, *Star*?" I asked.

"Oh, I hate that," she said, wincing. She leaned closer, like she wanted to girl gab with me.

"So how 'bout those new tits on Jackie? How much ya think she paid for them?"

"I really don't know, Starla. I didn't think to ask."

Of course I knew. Jackie had shared every last detail, even going so far as to ask my help on background checking the doctor. But that was between Jackie and me. Not Starla, who watched Jackie across the showroom work her magic on another bickering couple.

"Oh! Looks like my customer came back. Gotta go," she said, running as fast as she could in her six-inch stripper heels.

Finally, some peace. I pulled up the website for L.A. City College and found they still had room in their upcoming accounting classes. Could I pull this off another semester? I'd nearly killed myself last time, juggling school and work and trying to pay for the damn tuition. But if I didn't want to answer phones at Beverly Hills Motors for the rest of my life, I needed to get a degree in something more useful than art.

"Hey."

It was Jackie, and she'd scared the crap out of me.

"Damn. You okay?" she asked.

I lowered my voice and looked around. "I was checking out the class schedule at City College."

"Oh, awesome. Hey, I was thinking about your comment earlier today. I still want to help."

"What are you talking about?"

She cleared her throat and lowered her voice. "You know. About getting some."

She raised her eyebrows to make sure I was following..

When she was convinced I wasn't a total dolt, she continued. "There's this place. It's called The Agency." She held a white business card in her hand.

I reached for it, but she snapped it back.

"Give me a sec. I need to explain," she said. "If you call this place, the owner, Zenia, will help you, ya know, get back in the saddle." She finally handed over the card.

The only thing on it were the words *The Agency*, a website URL, and a local phone number.

All printed on some thick, high-quality card stock. Rich and creamy.

I flipped it over a few times in my fingers. "What is this? A dating service? Like Match.com?"

She looked around again, and only when she saw that the boss was on the other side of the showroom, did she continue. "No, that's not what it is. It's an...um...escort agency."

An escort agency... when Jackie said get back in the saddle, she wasn't joking.

"Oh. Well. Thanks. But I'm not interested in dating women. You know that's not my thing."

I pushed the card back toward her. She wouldn't take it.

"No, dummy," she said. I mean, I knew I needed to get some action. But *escorts*? "They don't have *female* escorts," she clarified. "They have *male* escorts."

No freaking way. How did a male escort service even exist? I mean, did women really hire…*dudes*?

"Well, I'm not sure that's the thing for me. And it's probably really expensive, anyway."

"You're right about that. It's not cheap. That's why I got you a gift certificate. I've already arranged it all with the owner, Zenia."

"You *what?*"

I looked around. Shit, I'd been loud, but the showroom was mostly empty, thank god.

"You *what?*" I repeated, whispering. "Why?"

She took a deep, patient breath. "Take the card home with you. Just think about it."

"I suppose you've done this before?" I asked.

She nodded and a huge smile spread across her face.

"Sure. Every now and then I want something a little different. The Agency always fits the bill. So to speak." She winked with great flair. "Oh, a customer. Gotta run."

She hustled across the showroom floor and out the door onto the lot, the smile never fading from her face.

Read more of Belle's story…

The Anti-Hero Chronicles
Dirty Game / Audio

Nasty Bet / Audio
Filthy Deal / Audio

**The Savage Mountain
Men Reverse Harem Series**
The Captive / Audio
The Runaway / Audio
The Pursued / Audio
The Prize / Audio
Boxset books 1-4 / Audio

Contemporary Reverse Harem
The Inheritance / Audio
The Renovation / Audio
The Promotion / Audio
The Gallery / Audio
The Collection / Audio
Boxset books 1-5

A Player Romance series 1-3
Mister Hollywood
Mister Fake Date
Mister Wrong

Billionaire Duet 1-2
Dirty Little Secret
Sinful Little Betrayal

STAY IN THE KNOW

Join my Insider Group
Exclusive access to private release specials, giveaways, the opportunity to receive advance reader copies (ARCs), and other random musings.

LET'S KEEP IN TOUCH
Mika Lane Newsletter
Email me
Visit me! www.mikalane.com
Friend me! Facebook
Pin me! Pinterest
Follow me! Twitter
Laugh with me! Instagram

Dear Reader:

Please join my Insider Group and be the first to hear about giveaways, sales, pre-orders, ARCs, and other cool stuff: http://mikalane.com/join-mailing-list.

Writing has been a passion of mine since, well, forever (my first book was "The Day I Ate the Milkyway," a true fourth-grade masterpiece). These days, steamy romance, both dark and funny, gives purpose to my days and nights as I create worlds and characters who defy the imagination. I live in magical Northern California with my own handsome alpha dude, sometimes known as Mr. Mika Lane, and an evil cat named Bill. These two males also defy my imagination from time to time.

A lover of shiny things, I've been known to try to new recipes on unsuspecting friends, find hiding places so I can read undisturbed, and spend my last dollar on a plane ticket somewhere.

I have several titles for you to choose from including the perennially favorite Billionaire and Reverse Harem stories. And have you see my Player Series about male escorts who make the ladies of Hollywood curl their toes and forget their names? Hottttt.... And my brand new anti-hero/mafia books are coming out in audio as I write this.

Exciting news: in June 2020, I will be publishing with Vi Keeland's and Penelope Ward's Cocky Hero Club as one of their contributing authors. Stay tuned for more on this or follow my Facebook page: https://www.facebook.com/mikalaneauthor. And, as if that's not cool enough, I am also writing in K. Bromberg's Everyday Heroes world. Look for that later in the year.

I'll always promise you a hot, sexy romp with kick-ass but imperfect heroines, and some version of a modern-day happily ever after.

I LOVE to hear from readers when I'm not dreaming up naughty tales to share. Join my Insider Group so we can get to know each other better http://mikalane.com/join-mailing-list, or contact me here: https://mikalane.com/contact.

xoxo
   Love,
   Mika